PETER HEAV

MW00723694

ALTAR OF THE MUSES

Copyright © Peter Heavenheld 2010
All rights reserved
First published worldwide by Peter Heavenheld Publishing 2010

Amateurs and professionals are hereby warned that *Hearts of Marble, Wills of Clay* and *Voyage without Charts* are subject to royalties. Both plays are fully protected under the copyright laws of the Commonwealth of Australia, the United Kingdom, the United States of America, and all countries covered by the Berne Convention or with which the above countries have reciprocal copyright arrangements. All rights, including professional and amateur performance, motion picture, television, internet, radio broadcasting, recitation, lecturing, public reading, and the rights of translation into foreign languages, are strictly reserved.

All enquiries concerning rights should be addressed to Peter Heavenheld through his Facebook™ page.

This is a work of fiction. No resemblance is intended to actual persons or events. Circumstances surrounding the death of Captain James Cook have been altered for dramatic effect.

This book is sold subject to the condition that it shall not, by way of trade or otherwise, be lent, resold, hired out, or otherwise circulated without the author's prior consent in any form of binding or cover other than that in which it is published and without a similar condition being imposed on the subsequent purchaser.

Heavenheld, Peter, 1980-
Altar of the Muses
ISBN 9780646527215

Cover design by Vladalahara
www.vladalahara.com

For Alexandra

About the Playwright

Peter Heavenheld was born in 1980 and grew up in Europe, Australia and the Pacific. He fell in love with the theatre during his university days, where he wrote, directed and starred in a sketch revue, *True Words from False Teeth*, and also acted in several other productions. He currently works in Canberra as a political and economic analyst. When not writing for work or pleasure, he enjoys music, cinema, travel, working out and fast cars.

Contents

Foreword

There is an extraordinary beauty and power in Elizabethan tragedy that continues to enthral. Action, revenge and violence jostle complex characterisation, deep introspection and rich poetry. The works of Shakespeare and Marlowe especially are grand canvases that show life in every colour of its misery, comedy and glory.

Many have sought to explain our fascination with tragedy. According to legend, the word 'tragedy' derives from the Greek phrase 'goat song,' perhaps recognising the chanted nature of early performances of tragedy; or perhaps establishing the contrast between the heights of poetry and the depths of our most lustful, animal instincts. For Aristotle, tragedy acted as a form of psycho-social catharsis enabling us to free the angst trapped inside us. Nietzsche saw tragedy as exposing the conflict between our Dionysiac lust to destroy and our Apollonic desire to create.

Tragedy is all of these and more – it illustrates mortality, greatness and the error that leads to the fall. All of these are fundamentally human characteristics. We all die. We all have the potential for greatness, but few of us realise it because we commit errors or merely miss opportunities. The error of the tragic hero is thus a metaphor for the mistakes we commit in the course of our life, the collective historical mistakes of humanity, and for some, the Christian concept of punishment for primordial sin.

Classical tragedy combines this primeval sense of mortality, doom and redemption with the loftiest poetry, as if to show that there is innate beauty in everything, no matter how depressing or sordid. That is why tragedy is arguably the highest expression of literature, and in its broadest sense, perhaps the highest expression of any form of art if we include vanitas paintings, Pieta statues and requiems.

Let these plays stand as a humble attempt to show posterity that our age, too, was conscious of how suffering and greatness can reflect each other.

Peter Heavenheld
June 2010

HEARTS OF MARBLE, WILLS OF CLAY

Tragedy in 5 Acts

"Make a mark within this world so that there is less for Death to erase."

Pliny the Younger

"Beware all thieves and imitators of other people's labour and talents who lay their audacious hands on our work."

Albrecht Dürer

"We are the blocks of stone from which the sculptor makes the men. The blows of the chisel which hurt us so much make us perfect."

C. S. Lewis

DRAMATIS PERSONAE

ORSEO VALENTINI di MANIERI, a sculptor of Florence
MARC'ETTORE "MARCO" MARGOLI, his friend
VIGILIA, a blind girl
BIANCA de CRISTOBALDI, a wealthy Maeceness
FIORENTINA de CRISTOBALDI, her daughter
MARIA, Orseo's landlady
A CAPTAIN in Bianca's employ
A GUILDSMAN (to be doubled with above)
Guards, Servants, a Messenger

Act I

Scene 1

[A sculptor's studio lit by one window. Marble statues of gods, goddesses, heroes and heroines in all sizes crowd it in various states of completion. A few items to one side indicate domestic life and indigence – a simple table, old chairs, a battered bed. ORSEO – young, thin and morose – lies on it, obscured. Enter a GUILDSMAN with a scroll. He bangs his staff thrice upon the floor.]

GUILDSMAN:
In the name of the *Arte di Pietra e Legname*[1] of Florence! Orseo Valentini di Manieri, the Council of the Masters of the Guild hath judged thou hast transgressed these edicts of our Charter: [Unrolls scroll] "That any marble used for internal decoration or sculpting is to be bought from the Guild, the Guild alone, and no other merchant irrespective of their repute, to prevent the hostility and mutual debasement sparked by the rub of competition..."

ORSEO:
[Rising] What!?

GUILDSMAN:
"That no member of the Guild shall work at night, for fear the dismal light may impair his workmanship, and also for fear that it would disadvantage those members of the Guild who keep more Christian hours..."

ORSEO:
Ha!

---

[1] "Guild of Stone and Timber," encompassing architects, masons, carpenters and sculptors

5

GUILDSMAN:
"That no member of the Guild is to produce more than four larger-than-life-sized carvings, or ten smaller-than-life-sized ones in any given day…"

ORSEO:
I was inspired! Canst thou not understand?
Oh God! How can I keep to common hours
Or stop myself at sculptures four just when
My spirit's lost within a giddy dance?
When I'm inspired, my brain's a busy hive
That's honeying with thoughts and heeds nought else!

GUILDSMAN:
"That the width of the shoulders of a male figure is not to be more than the distance from the navel to the top of the head…"

ORSEO:
For narrow minds on narrow shoulders roost?

GUILDSMAN:
"That the lowest price of a statue over five feet in height is not to fall below two florins, so as to provide all sculpting members of the Guild with a fair price…"

ORSEO:
But I was starving! I was glad to pounce
On any price that crawled into my path!

GUILDSMAN:
"That no member of the Guild is to use a method or a tool unknown to others without publicly sharing it with all other members."
[Rolls up scroll]

ORSEO:
Thy breed of dunce would wonder at the thought
That there are even other methods, let alone

Attempt to catch and harness them for use.

GUILDSMAN:
The Council of the Masters of the Guild
Hath found thee punishable on these counts.
Thou art to be expelled from out the Guild
And stripped of all thy privilege forthwith.

ORSEO:
Then what am I to do? How will I live?

GUILDSMAN:
The Council also will apply unto
The Magistrate of Florence thee to have debarred
From practicing as sculptor in this town.

ORSEO:
May those pusbags melt in Hell's confoundry!
Methinks I'll pilgrim unto other towns,
And settle in a place that merits me.

GUILDSMAN:
In that case it's my duty to unchain
A dreadful warning from its cryptic cave.
There is a clause not in the Charter writ
That to protect the members of the Guild,
And all the skills that they are wardens of,
If any member, current or expelled,
Hints threats to bare the secrets of the Guild
To artisans in other towns or lands,
The Guild's been granted legal rights to set
Assassins onto all such reprobates.

ORSEO:
I cannot credit that!

GUILDSMAN:
                    I speak the truth.

ORSEO:

Nor art nor morals have a vote
When peril's cries debate thy hypocritic fees
And farcical decrees. No, anything
To keep the pharisaic sanctity
Of thy fat treasure chests inviolate!
Thy Guild reduces th' hearts of Man and Art
To charted works of regulated parts,
Creation for the market clubbed and plucked.
Go buy thine hushed assassins, kill what's left
With minions who'll chain Prometheus!
Then may they turn on thee instead! I fear them not!
Aroint, hyena of the heinous kind!

GUILDSMAN:

Thine answer's noted and will be conveyed.
In the name of the *Arte di Pietra e Legname* of
[Florence!

[Bangs staff thrice, and exit GUILDSMAN.]

ORSEO:

This gadfly could not breathe if th' act were not
Secured upon his precious Charter's page!
I still recall one gilded fool who did
With scrutiny one of my statues prod.
He said, "You cannot make a finger thus."
"Why not?" I asked him back. "Because," quoth he,
"No one has made a finger thus before."
"What is the harm if I do make it now?"
"'Twill point out those who make no other kind,"
Came his reply. One mass, one thought, one way…

[Lies. A pause. Enter MARCO, elegantly dressed after the
fashion of the age]

MARCO:

Orseo! Orseo! I bring thee good tidings!
I've just effected the most gainful sale

8

Of *Venus* to a visiting Marquis.

ORSEO:
[aside] Pander to the oily classes…

MARCO:
                    He was
Resplendently delighted with her shape
As well as execution, and lent voice
(In words of staunch conviction) t' a desire
To purchase for himself more of thy works
On his sequent visits here to Florence.
For shame, art thou awake or do my words
Wash over thee like aimless raindrops? Hark!
A statue sold! Is it not wonderful?
For Heaven's sake, art thou not drunk with joy?
Why must thou keep good humour from thy side
As if it were a beggar wracked with plague?
One of thy statues I have just retailed.
The first in many moons, and thou saith naught?
Orseo!

ORSEO:
         For what sum?
[A pause]

MARCO:
               A quarter florin.

ORSEO:
[Rising] How? A quarter? O, thou cozened gull-head!
The marble in 't alone was worth a better part!
A quarter? Heard I right? In faith, a fool
And blackguard are both stuffed into thy skin!

MARCO:
Let thy reason here prevail. 'Tis little –

9

ORSEO:
It is unpardonably paltry!

MARCO:
Peace!
I know 'tis little, but upon my word,
Heracles had a task less wearying
In questing Keryneia's nimble deer
Than I've had with elusive customers!
I had to set a lower blank in price
To catch those offers that had passed below.

ORSEO:
Perchance the flaw abides in thee instead,
For that *Venus* was sunlit perfection,
Reflected in at least two florins' shine.

MARCO:
Orseo, I'm thy most devoted friend.
Much effort I expend to mart thy work.
'Tis not my fault the wealthy want them not!

ORSEO:
What can one purchase for a florin's fourth?
A crack of bread? A gob of cheese? O fie!
I would do better if I'd come to carve
From mozzarella, not from marble, or,
Perchance, collect my teeth as they vault out
When I in famine sink, and try to scratch
Some scrimshaw into them, like scurvied sailors do!

MARCO:
I shall apply my firmest of resolve
To sell yet more. But now the season's out.
Most noted families forsake the town
And cool on country villas' colonnades,
Their city mansions ceded to the heat.
When they return, the weathervanes their compass,

Then errant Fortune shall come back to thee.

ORSEO:
The *popolo minuto*[2] for the minute lives,
And taste to them inhabits only food.
They carve but joints, not stone. What's art to them?
Elaboration that's not worth th' expense.
They can nor recognise nor fathom it.
They trickle through this life, unknowing crowds,
To drain into a pothole at its end.
The *popolo grassi,*[3] who could if but they would,
Elect instead to lavish untold wealth
Upon their divan-draping courtesans,
And then their petty, posing rivalries,
And then their games of hazard, played to prove
Adventure's mane upon the mildest men,
And only then, if there is aught unspent
Will it be grudging rolled towards us artisans.
Even then, 'tis prickly with conditions:
Commands to flatter tap-shaped noses' forms,
To lie politely of some coddish eyes.
The spirit's trapped amongst their narrow bounds!
O they whose minds can soar and can attain
The lofty turrets of true masterworks,
And who are manumised from mundane chains
Like th' insufficiency of wherewithal,
Or pressing urge t' expend the fill of it
On sating the satyr entrapped in them,
They rival unicorns in rarity!

MARCO:
Thy thronging troubles could be vanquished all
If thou wouldst take commissions.

---

[2] Literally 'minute people' – Florence's working class
[3] Literally 'fattened people' – Florence's ruling class

ORSEO:

That I won't!
I am an artist, not a soldier. No,
The purest of expressions floats on rainbow wings.
It can't be made to march in muddy ruts
That lavish carriages behind them plough.
Besides, commissions are forbidden now,
When serpents of so tortuous events
Are strangling me, like Laocoon and his sons.

MARCO:
What dost thou say?

ORSEO:

That I am fresh expelled,
Nay, excommunicated from that cult
Of cloistered minds who worship wealth
And make a ritual of the conventional.

MARCO:
The Guild?

ORSEO:
Aye, those dolts.

MARCO:

What calamity!
Thy craft is beached out of the current's flow,
Nor canst thou buy supplies for newer fleets.
How will we navigate this reef of bans?

ORSEO:
O what serve words when I breathe only them,
Yet cannot spirit into stone suspire?
Nor funds, nor marble, and the harshest check:
Mine inspiration's bird nests elsewhere.
All fonts of sustenance dry up at once…

[Lies]

MARCO:
But not the font of friendship whence we drink!
To get so much bestraught becomes thee not.
All here into completion's comfort settles.
Here Pegasus and beau Bellerophon
Seem ready now to ring the moon, whilst there
Actaeon's hounds in malice grin their fangs
T' revolt like malcontents against their lord.

ORSEO:
Misshapen effigies.

MARCO:
                         Thou misprize them!
In aspect they are bristlingly alive.
But tell me what grand plans thou labour'st o'er
To set afloat upon thy fancy's sea?
What will be th' next great *chef d' oeuvre*?

ORSEO:
                                        I know not!

MARCO:
The nature of thy mind's to mill and grind
To turn and turn with clockwork constancy.
There must be some conception thawing into form!
Come, what wilt thou do?

ORSEO:
                         Sleep, so leave me be.

MARCO:
That I shan't! All reason cries in protest
To see such greatness idle in malaise.
Squeeze ev'ry hour for all its minutes' juice
And pour them through the filter of thy skill
Into a fresh cascade of sinews sinuous!
[A pause]

A sagittary thou hast never tried,
Though there's a subject with a wondrous form
To parry ev'ry common sculpting thrust.
Canst thou see the fabled equine corpus
Upon which stands the tower of man's soul?
The savage might and freedom of the one
Is tempered with the other's sage divinity,
More perfect so as one than each alone.
I've never seen one yet depicted true.
When painted, their forms slip in oils.
What saith thou to it?

       ORSEO:
              Silence.
       MARCO:
                  So be it.
Might I suggest instead Prometheus,
Who stole for us invention's sacred spark?
He promiseth us opportunities!
Methinks it would be modest to include
A precious stone to signal th' ember's fire...
But no. I see the thought warms not thy frost.
What then? If I were ruler o'er this rocky race...
Then what I'd wish for most would be... 'twould be a
                                [bride.

A figure standing lone, a simple pose,
In spirit and dimension true to life.
Venus, as thou said, was sunlit in perfection,
Yet also, as the Marquis rightly said,
Of practical proportion for all tours,
And blanketed with ease amongst his shirts.
Build me now an unabbreviated one,
An edifice to female beauty true!

       ORSEO:
I've pondered of a goddess of full length.

MARCO:
Then ponder it some more! Direct at it
Thy burning arrows of imagining
And set the thought alight! I wish to see
The hammer and the chisel growing both
Into thine hands in tireless mastery!

ORSEO:
It can't be done!

MARCO:
                    Why not, in Heaven's name?

ORSEO:
I pray thee, part. [Coughs] Each word is anguish to spit
                                                    [out.
MARCO:
Why can't thou dress a goddess into stone?

ORSEO:
The face...

MARCO:
          None frowned upon thy work before.

ORSEO:
Nay, list, I lack a model for the face.
The body, that is fancy's easy play.
The face, however, needs humanity,
Reality that cannot be surmised.
The face must touch the soul. Its piety
Half-glimpsed within a convent garden's shade,
Its languor caught in pool-reflection's empty dance,
Its beauty by a corbelled window fleeting framed...
More detail limns the physiognomy
Than all the rest – such delicate contours,
An equilibrium elusive as a dream!
And that is why a pattern I so pressing need.

MARCO:
I know a hand to fit that velvet glove…

ORSEO:
O, that will help me naught! What will she earn?
A bread-loaf's half?

MARCO:
               We'll trample ramparts all!
If this piece promises t' eclipse the rest,
We'll let no cloud o'er Earth efface its glow!

ORSEO:
Mayhap my hope's lost locket glimmers yet.
Thou art a friend most true… Yet how we prate!
'Tis marble that I need! Material!
The gravid mass of practicality
To anchor fantasy that flits about.

MARCO:
Indeed. Whence marble? For a statue unto life
Thou'lt need a most Olympian of blocks.
Troop, my thoughts, and charge that rub – I have it!
The antique Villa Fiesola's ruins,
A stone's mere throw beyond the city walls.
Those grounds are grave unto such column trunks,
And all of choicest Northern marble carved.

ORSEO:
'Tis thy design to steal a block from there?

MARCO:
It is a most extensive ruin. Tell me,
Who'd miss a single tree from acres o' wood?

ORSEO:
A column section weighs a Papal mass.
We'll want the force to budge it e'en an inch!

MARCO:
I am acquainted with a family
Of dockside packers who can carry anything
Except for conversation's cumbrous lines.
We'll have them heave it (under night's inked cape)
Upon a cart and bid them bring the guest
Up to thy chamber in an owlish hour.

ORSEO:
Now?

MARCO:
Now. As ripe a time as any, is it not?
[Goes to window]
See, Artemis drops not her veil of fog.
This cloak of darkness is most opportune,
For in its pocket hides the key t' unlock our scheme.

ORSEO:
No, Marco. Hold. I cannot quit my rooms.
To do so is a well of anguish too profound.
Th' uncertainty of spaces gaping wide,
The choking company of unknown men,
And worst of all some fraughtage porters... No!

MARCO:
Thou cannot nourish fear with them! All four
Are stricken with a silence without peer,
A peace they breach but seldom in a year.
I witnessed how one dropped upon his foot
A leaden crate and not a sigh expelled.
To assure thee firmer yet, I'll style thee
A foreign baron of superb repute
Who hates with venom ev'ry word he hears
That skips off tongues in local dialect.

ORSEO:
I quiver at the spectral vision's thought

17

That is yon villa garden's void expanse.

MARCO:
'Tis night, Orseo. We will take with us
A lantern with the warming glow of home.
Beyond its magic sphere all beasts will fade,
Be they creations of or flesh or mind.

ORSEO:
Nay, hold. I've chanced upon a better course.
Why goest thou not as mine ambassador?
Thou hast the foundations of the craft.
I've taught thee ample skill to spall the stone.
It can't have withered yet! Go in my stead.

MARCO:
A talent mean as mine needs more than crumbs
To feed it to some semblance of ability.
For how will I know which stone is the best?
Such enterprise, like tasting wine, requires
An Epicure's capacity to choose.

ORSEO:
'Tis true.

MARCO:
    Wilt thou now deign to join the hunt?

ORSEO:
Aye. With th' reluctance of a rusty hinge.

MARCO:
My friend, those words delight me endlessly!
I'll race ahead those porters to engage.
Gather all thine instruments and follow!

[Exit MARCO, then ORSEO]

Scene 2

[Later that night. The studio is dark and empty. Groans
offstage. A large block of marble is pushed onstage. Enter
ORSEO. He collapses onto the couch, coughing. Enter
MARCO]

MARCO:
My friend, thou art afflicted grievously.

ORSEO:
'Tis but the icy fingers of the wind
That grip my throat.

MARCO:
      I counsel thee to take
That never-failing remedy: a rest.

ORSEO:
'Tis trivial. I am restored.
[Gets up, lights candle and touches the marble block.]
       What Greek
Or Roman master did adorn thee so,
To proudly hold a canopy, like Atlas did,
Above our mortal insignificance?
Stood Thou the tests of angry centuries
In thy integrity, if not thy post.
How toppled Thou off thy pedestal's height
To lie, a conquered giant, in the grass?
Now Thou art poised to be reborn afresh,
Though like a royal surgeon's hand mine shakes
To meddle with a chip of history,
To rough again what greater hands have smoothed.
[Begins to carve with vigour. MARCO lies.]

MARCO:
I am rejoiced our honoured visitor
Has prised thee from ill humour's vice.

19

ORSEO:
Unto a sculptor, th' unsullied, virgin rock
Is his vocation's altar most sublime.
On 't we say mass, but not with book and candle,
But with meissel and mallet.

MARCO:
                              Orseo,
Why is 't that thou eschew all company?

ORSEO:
It is the reasoned mind's response to th' world,
For people are so wretched, stunted inside out,
They're nothing and aspire to nothing more.
They tick-like search for faults of character
On which to their advantage they can bite.
What use are they to me? Their lies, greed, lust?
Here amongst these statues is a world more perfect.
Here's order, beauty and eternity.
Nor looks of censury, nor words of curse.

MARCO:
And neither have they souls.

ORSEO:
                              In faith, they do!
Puffs of my soul have entered each of them!
Look on these limbs and features that describe
Th' intricate mosaics of expression.
Do they not speak to thee? Do they not seem to live
With th' intensity of Nature's arching flesh
Within their moment caged by time and stone?
Besides, why need I others when I have
The fortune of a friend such as thyself
Who eases me o' that abhorrent chore:
Converting flexing rock to flattened gold,
For I could never feign against myself
Enough indifference for what I make

20

To suffer selling it. Whene'er I tried
It stunk of harlotry, or fouler still,
'Twas like my children I was slaving off.
One good friend makes up for all th' foes that teem
Beyond the boundary of these four walls.
True friendship that's devoid of any aim
To profit from another is so nobly rare,
And friendship's state is more preferable
To hollow loneliness in solitude
Or quelling loneliness in multitude.
The company of one who shares one's thoughts,
Understands half-words, and reads all humours...
Is not that need as clamouring and simple
As is the one for water's juice of life?
'Tis a part that parents, spouses, masters
Or fellow guildsmen cannot aptly act.
Friendship represents the recognition
Of commonality that is unique,
A constancy pervading faith and time,
A bond that holds, no matter what assails
Or one or both. The solace o' fellowship
Deserves kind nurture like a growing tree
Which will become a refuge from the storms of life.
A friend lends counsel in incertitude,
Support in need and strength in unity,
Duality within the duel of life.
Here's wassail from Aristotle's cup of wisdom,
That "Friendship is composed of but one soul
Inhabiting two bodies."

     MARCO:
          Thanks.

     ORSEO:
          But no!
'Tis thou who merits most the meagre gift
That grateful words extend for want of else.
Thou brought me cheer since we two were mere boys

Playing midst my late father's bricking-kilns,
And now I thank thee with sincerity
For this grand stone that means the Earth to me.

MARCO:
There is one ill no friendship saves me from.
[Yawns]
It bears the appellation "weariness."
Dost thou intend to labour through the night?

ORSEO:
Do I recall thy voice exhorting me:
"Squeeze ev'ry hour for all its minutes' juice?"

MARCO:
True, yet what of thy spell of faint before?

ORSEO:
Stone I need like bread, and stone I knead like dough.
I hungered then, but now this is a feast
That fat Lucullus would Olympus deem.
I am an Antaeus whom Mother Earth
Reanimates each time he touches her.

MARCO:
Mine eyelids are exhaust to fight for light...
[Rises. A clock strikes in the distance.]
It is the second hour of the morn.
Day creeping comes when I've not paid the tax
Of yesterday with rest, so here's adieu.
Tomorrow... nay, today, I'll seek thee out
A copy whom to sculpt.

ORSEO:
                              Fetch me some courtesan,
But with a countenance of a goddess worth.
The body's state is immaterial,
Whether 'tis chewed to bone by hunger's fangs

Or rotting as a swamp of basest vice.
The physiognomy skills most.

MARCO:
$$\text{Good night.}$$

[Exit MARCO. The stage darkens.]

Scene 3

[Later in the morning. ORSEO has worked through the night.
Enter MARCO, leading VIGILIA.]

MARCO:
Orseo, list. This maid's Vigilia.

ORSEO:
Orseo Valentini di Manieri.

VIGILIA:
Is there just one of you?

ORSEO:
$$\text{What dost thou say?}$$

VIGILIA:
You've names enough for two at least.

MARCO:
$$\text{In faith!}$$

[She moves uncertainly towards ORSEO's voice.]

ORSEO:
Oh! She sees not!

VIGILIA:
                Yet she the better hears.

MARCO:
Thou needst a model, not a crow's-nest watch.

ORSEO:
She'll not see the sculpture!

VIGILIA:
                    She will see it
In her own way. She also has a name.

[VIGILIA moves cautiously, until she reaches a statue. She feels it with delicate touch, then moves to the next.]

ORSEO:
Who is this girl?

MARCO:
             Again, what matters it?
She is a willing copy for thine art.
Think'st thou the face is right?

ORSEO:
                     'Tis adequate.

[The last in VIGILIA's line is ORSEO himself. She "observes" him.]

VIGILIA:
Oh! This one's not as well made as the rest.

MARCO:
Vigilia is much the jester.

VIGILIA:
              Aye,

24

A jester, but no fool. For if I weren't,
I'd be upon a madness wild impaled.
When spiteful Fate has spat one in both eyes
One must perceive the world for what it is.
I cannot cry, perforce I have to laugh.

MARCO:
Let us commence the rite we're gathered for.
Seat here thyself, beside this window's glance.

[MARCO places a chair by the window and guides her into it.
ORSEO begins carving the face. MARCO lies upon the couch.]

VIGILIA:
Pray, hold. I wish to see 't.

ORSEO:
The statue?

VIGILIA:
Aye.

Lead forth.

[Examines it with touch]

ORSEO:
What think'st thou of it?

VIGILIA:
Adequate.

ORSEO:
'Tis yet unborn, unfinished, forming still!
Observe it when 't emerges like a pearl
From its present shell of rocky roughness.

VIGILIA:
What goddess will she be?

25

ORSEO:

                    I know not yet.

[VIGILIA sits. ORSEO begins, reluctantly. A pause.]

        VIGILIA:
Why does the ghost of silence haunt this room?

        ORSEO:
What ghost?

        VIGILIA:
                I like it more when people speak.
As one deprived of sight, I doubly feel
The solitude of stillness, that void cell
Where doubts begin that others e'en exist.

        ORSEO:
My trimming tools speak richer tones than words,
In harmonies I wish t' articulate.
[Another pause]

        VIGILIA:
Then speak you, Marco. Tell me what you will.
You said such wondrous things of yesterday.
I trust you have not spent a wealth of words
And left your purse a pauper for more speech?
Your charging words invaded all my thoughts,
And reinforcement now demand.

        MARCO:
                    Marry –

        ORSEO:
No. Words are breathed out as the air gone stale,
And never ought return.

VIGILIA:
Stale thoughts only,
The freshest ones feel like a fragrant breeze.
[Yet another pause. ORSEO sighs.]
Your sighs are wrapt in melancholia.

ORSEO:
I should have perseveréd yesternight.
Today the magic hath diffused.

VIGILIA:
I feel
So like a dame, my portrait done in marble.

ORSEO:
Prithee, peace! I crave quiet when I carve.

VIGILIA:
And I am craven when it's quiet! Come,
What if I grant you leave to question me
Of anything at all that you would know?
I'll keep afloat above the emptiness...

ORSEO:
Who art thou?

VIGILIA:
I have never seen myself.

ORSEO:
What is thy living?

VIGILIA:
Not to die.

ORSEO:
Whence hail thee from?

VIGILIA:

               A womb. And you?

ORSEO:

How knowest Marco?

VIGILIA:

               Passing well.

ORSEO:

Where dost thou dwell?

VIGILIA:

               In endless night.

ORSEO:

Why let my queries answers fish
When they catch only oily eels?

VIGILIA:

Ah, Nature plays her impish games...
[ORSEO works in silence]
      Am I condemned for audience to naught
      But the gentle patter of a hammer?
      Too loud for rain, too wrong of rhythm to be
      The smithy of a heart. I plead you, talk.
      Throw pebbling words to ripple this dead calm.

ORSEO:

What's there to say?

VIGILIA:

               Your first, most instant thought.
[ORSEO blows on the statue, and begins to cough violently.]

ORSEO:

What is this croak that's lodged within my pipe?

28

MARCO:
[Rising] Thy body's hoarse advice to gain some rest.
Thou art most out of sorts today. We'll go.

ORSEO:
No, Marco, stay. 'Tis from the morning frost,
The warming sun has not yet mounted noon's high
                                                    [saddle
MARCO:
Vigilia is lacking time.

ORSEO:
                    For what?

MARCO:
'Tis time for us to part, for thee to couch.
Thou art most ill, and I'm most firm, so rest thou wilt.
Thou hast not bridged with sleep the gap twixt days,
And Nature cannot wade through muddled hours.
This way, Vigilia.

VIGILIA:
                    Adieu, good sir.

ORSEO:
O what a fruitless, wintered day is this!

[Exeunt MARCO and VIGILIA. ORSEO lies upon his couch.
The stage darkens.]

Scene 4

[The following day. ORSEO still on his couch. Enter MARCO and VIGILIA.]

MARCO:
Orseo! Here's a dose of tidings fain!
The Duchess o' Bevilaqua
Desires to see *Poseidon*. I'm due
At her palazzo in but half an hour.
Methinks we've charmed ourselves another patron!
The Duchess is associated well,
An arbiter of taste in many spheres
Whose sun the lesser nobles orbit close.
If she can be enticed to favour thee,
'Twill gain admittance for thy works
To countless chambers o' finest elegance.
I'll leave thee with Vigilia. Farewell,
And study thoughts to armour me with luck!

ORSEO:
Thanks, Marco, and farewell.

[Exit MARCO]

But welcome, muse!
[ORSEO gets up and guides her by the hand.]
Come, run thy pretty hands o'er it again.
This stone of the philosopher will be
As true to life as is the naked babe.
That is this marble's noble destiny.
[Seats her and begins to carve with passion.]

VIGILIA:
You are so changed, I can uneath distinguish you!
It is as though you live a doubled life.

ORSEO:
Life's purpose must be some reverse of Death,
For if it is not, it will be instead
A purpose somehow aimed against itself,
Like a shot that cracks the cannon firing it.
But what could be that opposite? Perchance
'Tis happiness? No. Death ends happiness.
Though Death and grief are counterpoints to joy,
Its tune can never play beyond one's life.
Is it then freedom? When demise occurs,
The soul is freed and with the cosmos joins.
The state of freedom thus survives the siege of Death.
Are we not born though free and slow renounce
That attribute through living's simple act?
Through ev'ry promise, bargain, lie and kiss,
The subjugation of ourselves unto
The laws and customs of our land? And oft
To shed those laws, reclaim our liberty,
Means Death. Can freedom rule the lines to sketch
The Plan of Life if it constructs a crypt?
No, freedom is no better opposite.
The truest antonym to Death must be
No other word but Immortality,
And one that is through great creation gained.
It can continue past its owner's end,
It is an exaltation of one's soul,
And Immortality's the highest truth,
For God creates and God is ever-lived,
Therefore Creation and Eternity
Divinely complement each other.

VIGILIA:
                                        Faith,
Methought that Marco was an orator.
He has a silver tongue, but yours is gold!

ORSEO:
Originality's my sweetest muse.

31

What is in drab predictability,
Being quotidian as clock-hands' paths
And joining crowds of kine, or thinking in
Dull aphorisms like a parrot stricken mute?
I spurn the specious and the simular!
Uniqueness in originality
Is th' force that lurches mankind on its way
To better and more elevated times.
From ere we towered Egypt's pyramids
As compass points towards the afterworld,
Or raised Hellenic columns' edifice
To the brightest perfection that mind can invent,
Or cleft in ev'ry land th' unfriendly clay
With Rome's imperial insignia,
Our rise has been in fitful starts and bounds
Fed by th' capricious yet unfailing trickle
Of thinkers who exceeded their own times,
Who rolled the millstone of their age ahead
Before expiring. And upon those stones
Yet others stood and built man closer unto God.
They numbered prophets, scholars, emperors,
Great generals, e'en artisans like me.
They wore no common qualities, save for
A brilliance of vision and a force of mind
That like a sunbeam rived through swirling dust
Which densed the air they found around themselves.
Originality's true luminance,
The lightning flash of sparkling prodigy
That glances off the gem of timelessness,
Such talent's mark of being chosen out by God
To be a prophet to the rest of men
And lead them to where none have dared before.
But how exiguous 'tis in the world!
A thimbleful is sprinkled over millions.
Thus many whittlers do but imitate
The graceful curves of Argive masterworks.
Low leeches on the veins of genius!
If Polyclitus quickened live today,

Would he oblige the expectations held
By fashioning the same Doryphoros?
No, he would give our sculptors something fresh
As an oasis that would make them gasp,
And choke upon the marble-dust they stir
Within the desert of their copying.
Yet it's not only my craft blighted so,
For many melodists do but repeat
The measures o' village dances, carnivals,
Ale-house songs. The base and thieving magpies!
Take as example that Brachimassi's Bolgar Songs
That on a crest of common favour kite,
(So much that even here I madness coast
From their too constant notes that climb from streets
Like whiffs of vendors' *carbonado* meats.)
The fools assume our friend Giovanni
Long laboured over those ear-trancing tunes,
Whereas he only toiled to scribble 'em down
With that vast diligence of fallow minds
Whose only merit's recognising where
The finest pearls are hid to be purloined,
Savouring, yet ne'er begetting th' essence
Of what makes greatness. He is music's shame,
And no composer to mine ears! Instead,
A non-composer. Non composer mentis! Ha!
[ORSEO breaks into another coughing fit. VIGILIA aids him to
the couch.]
But there's a fouler sort than his! The kind
That is dismayed by others' faculties
And will essay with spiteful jealousy
To denigrate and vandalise grand works!
Revise them, lower them to his crude breed!
[Collapses again with violent coughs.]

VIGILIA:
You must not fume such overheated words
That boil your choler, or 'tis you who'll choke
On th' marble-dust you stir.

33

ORSEO:

O chide me not!
And look not on me with such nursemaid care!
I am afire with inspiration's blast!
I'm doubly struck alive by Zeus' thunderbolt.

VIGILIA:
Your day will burst if filled yet more.
Rest.

ORSEO:
What? I am alike a man possessed!
I must erupt this force and channel it in stone!
I cannot halt upon momentum's peak!
I am now midway through a lengthy bound.
If thou depriv'st me of my work, I'll fall,
I'll headlong plunge into an abyss deep.
[ORSEO struggles, but suddenly stops to contemplate
VIGILIA.]
Thy face... appears to me angelic fair.

VIGILIA:
In faith, 'twas barely adequate before.

ORSEO:
I'm as inept with words as skilled with stone.
Forgive me, pray.

VIGILIA:
It cut, but is forgiv'n.
[ORSEO rises, then kisses the shaping statue.]

ORSEO:
Vigilia, know'st thou what I did then?

VIGILIA:
Your urgent tone implies I shall forthwith.

ORSEO:

I kissed thy face, but only its facsimile,
For I dare not profane with mortal touch
That most ambrosial original. I hope
I have Pygmalion's devotion to besiege
The Lord with such an orisons' deluge
That He will bless me with the selfsame grace
That Aphrodite shewed my counterpart.
And yet I dread to send those prayers' doves!
For if their physic grant is me denied,
I'll waste in lifeless shadow that's unlit
By thy celestial bright aureole.

VIGILIA:

I'm reft of words! They've fled like frighted fawns,
This unexpectedness has muted me.
Ere none has deemed me worth such compliment...

ORSEO:

You captivate me, sweet Vigilia.
Throughout my tired life I've beauty sought,
On surfaces and in profundities.
Now knowing you, my journey has arrived.
You are the tranquil forest lake that I,
The lost and weary traveller, have found.
Fair sunlight dances on the water's glass,
All Heaven is reflected in that shimmering,
And I can slake my thirst for beauty thence,
And inspiration's holy waters draw
To pour upon my talent's sainted fruit.
Yet far below the grace and sparkling wit
A brooding sorrow lurks in caverns dark.
That is your strange and wondrous beauty's source,
A dignified nobility of grief.
I long t' immerse myself within that depth
To quest for treasures I can raise from it,
And set a gem into each statue's heart.
Will you requite this love that has burst forth,

Like dolphin breaking through the yesty waves,
De profundis?

> VIGILIA:
> I know not what to say,
> My thoughts are tangled like a kitten's toy,
> For our acquaintance is scarce woven yet.

> ORSEO:
> Then I'll make you know me as if I'd been
> Enfolded in your mind since infant memory.
> Ask anything, leaf t' any page you will.
> I'll read my thoughts to you like verses o' love.

> VIGILIA:
> Marco forewarned me not of this.

> ORSEO:
> Where's he?
> Beyond the ring our touching hands create.

[Takes her hands]

> VIGILIA:
> Pray, stop. I beg you, leave me be.

> ORSEO:
> What's this?
> Art thou so cold that thou wilt spurn me thus?
> Dost thou not sense of how that sculpted form
> In spirit us unites like nuptial plights?
> How its creation links us in a harmony
> Not even crystal birds could sing?

> VIGILIA:
> No, halt!
> Perchance 't unites our spirits, but naught else.

ORSEO:
Why dost thou torment me with such indifference,
Nay, aversion?

VIGILIA:
I'm unprepared for this.
You stray to where the sunlight glimmers brief,
But shadows of regret long linger.

ORSEO:
Nay,
Such masterwork's completion consummates
Man's highest powers to conceive and make.
The best ideas must be brought to th' world
With same protracted pain as children's birth,
For grand ideas live, they live to grow
And flower and beget still grander ones!
These thoughts enthralled thee moments past.

VIGILIA:
They were orated then, not badly acted out.
[He struggles towards the couch with her.]
O cease!

ORSEO:
Why dost thou wriggle like a fresh-caught fish?
Most others would this lofty honour deem,
Yet thou gainsay it with such petulance!

VIGILIA:
Help!

ORSEO:
Dost thou not ache to further Nature's force
That froths and wells foudroyantly in me?
To be illumined by the heat and light
Of such an ember of Prometheus as I?
I am the agent of a mighty power

That surges, forges on relentlessly,
That charges with volcanic fury forth
Towards exalted perpetuity!
And now, I condescend from alpine peaks
To part my greatness with thee, raise thee up!
Canst thou not feel that power animating thee?
The sacred power to advance... beget... create!

[He suffers another attack of violent coughing. VIGILIA escapes.]

          VIGILIA:
Beast! Swine! 'Twas mating more than animating!
You're more a pig than a Pygmalion!
A villainous tatterdemalion,
Rank scoundrel moulded of the vilest mud!

[Exit VIGILIA crying. As she stumbles across the studio, she knocks a statue of the *Virgin* off its pedestal. ORSEO collapses.]

          ORSEO:
[Gasping] How comes my heart to be a race of hooves,
My lungs as bellows belching out my soul?
God sighs into our shell and we begin to pulse,
And then He breathes in and we expire.
Is 't how the all-sustaining spirit now
Abandons me?

[Enter MARCO]

          MARCO:
               My friend, what's ailing thee?

          ORSEO:
I'm robbed of breath... but mercifully it returns...

          MARCO:
How fell the *Virgin*? Where's Vigilia?

ORSEO:
She parted... early.

MARCO:
What, alone!?
With not a blesséd comet guiding her?
For shame, how couldst thou let her leave alone?
Why, there is a cannonade of dangers
That could o'ertake her! She may be assailed,
Or plunge into the Arno's flow,
Or flounder lost in city alleys' serried net!
Thou must have lost thy senses with thy breath
To let her go unaided. Is that skull
Inhabited by care for none but thee?
A gruntling keeps for others more concern!

ORSEO:
O cork that mouth that spills so much! And go.
I cannot bear nor sight, nor sound, nor thought
Of anyone. Betake thyself!

MARCO:
I shall!
Mayhap she can be rescued yet. Of this,
We shall speak yet.

[Exit MARCO]

ORSEO:
For stars I leapt, in mud I fell...

[The stage darkens.]

Act II

[Months later. The statue with Vigilia's face stands unfinished.
ORSEO is working on another one, chipping less than pausing.]

ORSEO:
Ponderous hours together melt for me
Into an indistinguishable mass,
A pointless flux: darkness, light; coldness, heat;
A bleak monotony of opposites
That chase each other to infinity…

[Enter MARCO]

MARCO:
I've traded it, Orseo!

ORSEO:
I am glad.

MARCO:
Go to! These tidings should revive thy cheer
As though they were a tumblerful of rum
In wintry gloom.

ORSEO:
They do just so. My thanks.

MARCO:
I traipsed through such adventures selling it.
I did accost His Reverence each time he chanced
To pause before some vendor's wares,
Until at last he galled into such rage
That he exprised the statue from my grip
To bring it down like Judgment Day upon my head.
Yet as he lifted it, his wrathed visage
Came level with th' marmoreal, at which,

40

Against his will, the drawstrings of his face
Loosed to the same display of saintliness
As th' one that thou depicted with such skill,
And with his face, his purse-cord slackened too.

ORSEO:
What estimation did he coin?

MARCO:
He... well...
I've troth that he will keenly ardent prove
To purchase other Holy statuary.

ORSEO:
I asked, how much?

MARCO:
Orseo, weigh the facts
Of what a valued client –

ORSEO:
Speak the price!

MARCO:
One florin.

ORSEO:
No...

MARCO:
Alack, 'twas all he gave.

ORSEO:
Didst thou not even try contending him
To stakes more golden?

MARCO:
I' faith! But he held firm,

With th' inexorable asperity
Of God's Commandment.

       ORSEO:

              Then I'm ruined!

       MARCO:
I shall assist thee with mine all through Fate's new
                                  [squall.
       ORSEO:
Am I a flea to have to ride on thee?
One florin! O, 'tis pelting little!
For what do I abrade myself to dust?
A sum to earn a famine-flavoured crust?
A loaf and cheese two months ago, and then
Another for a month, and now again...
The landlady's been vulturing me for my dues
For rings of weeks. What can I offer her?
A disused leg? And what of marble stores?
These mud-born cares intrude upon mine art.
Why am I cursed with skill so ill belittled?
Why is mine only chance to stir the world
A whirlpool pulling me to sure demise?
Why is the quill that writes my name in time
A poisoned point that signs and seals mine end?
Why was I not equipped with weaponry
More valued by our times? A merchant's greed,
A soldier's thoughtless valour, or perchance,
The sinful comeliness of one's who kept?
Why am I mercilessly forced to wade
Towards a ruin of health and state? Why? Why!?

       MARCO:
Orseo, if thy desperation would
But pierce thy pride! Thou couldst thy while carve up
Betwixt commissions and th' indulgence of
Unfettered free imagination.

42

ORSEO:

No!

MARCO:
Perchance thou couldst try one, observe its taste.
It may not be as bitter as thou think'st.
Experience oft makes the fairest judge.
At least 'twill sup thee through these direst times.
And fear thee not the Guild, I'll pass them by.

ORSEO:
I do not, cannot duck in palaces
And beautify in stone what is in flesh
Repulsive vile, to fake such "likenesses"
Which strive to cheat some chosen bridegroom's eye.
I'll not eat mine integrity for food!
What's more, we cannot hold a sitting here,
In this base attic, and not after...

MARCO:

What?

ORSEO:
To take commissions is apostasy,
A recantation of my precepts sworn.

MARCO:
What if thou never had to meet the model
And if she were a rare and noble rose
That's petalled round with beauty, grace and thought,
All to inspire thy too unwilling hands
To capture their unearthly trinity?
One who'd be worth the effort even if
No payment emphasised her loveliness?

ORSEO:
"If I never had to meet the model?"
How wilt thou mock impossibility?

Thou hopest to bridge the gap with easel-wood?
No portrait's fluency can ever vie
With Nature's marvellous reality.

MARCO:
I've whet thy curiousity! Now list.
Malgré reclusion, thou hast doubtless heard
The name "de Cristobaldi." They're amongst
Our city's wealthiest patrician families.
Bianca, matriarch of that famed line
Has uttered orders that she much desires
Her daughter Fiorentina sketched in marble.
For reasons veiled before our vulgar sort,
She has reserved the bust be set in stone
An orphan to its subject's know and sight.
That's marred away the foremost gallery
Of portraiters-in-stone like critic vitriol.
However, unbeknownst to them,
Fiorentina, mid her other virtues,
Wears her devoutness like an amulet,
And with her princess presence ornaments
The Cristobaldi chapel thrice a day.
There bound she promenades with frequency
The Via stretching like a waking cat below,
On which thy window winks from high.
Thou couldst hence carve her in mute secrecy.
Art not thy blunted senses tingled keen
By this oblique procedure's novelty?
'Twould daunt a lesser prodigy than thee.
What saith thou on 't?

ORSEO:
                              I have to view her first.
If thy description truly renders her,
I might agree.

MARCO:
                              Brave words! Where counts the clock?

[Leans through the window to look at the clock tower.]
When few more grains minutely down an hourglass
[drop,

Fiorentina de Cristobaldi
Will yonder ride along.

ORSEO:
She will be far,
And distance is to detail brutal foe.

MARCO:
My stars sit right today – naught baffles me!
I can drench tonic over ev'ry rub.
I have with me a wondrous instrument
Whose journey here from Gallic lands I did arrange.
It came for Leo, he's a Pisan friend,
A cultivator of the sciences.
The French refer to it as "téléscope,"
Though "dragon's eye" its powers better names.
It works the magic of elaborated glass
To snatch the stellar specks from nests in skies
And hatch them into beings large as eggs.
'Tis praised as pinnacle in scholarment
And means of sight, a Moses-rod t' astronomy.
Now Fiorentina it will hither bring.
The very thing to scan her features fair.
Methinks she comes! Make haste, Orseo. There!
[They look out through the window with the telescope.]

ORSEO:
Is she upon the milk-white steed?

MARCO:
Thy recognition admiration plain admits!

ORSEO:
Perchance it does…

MARCO:
                    Wilt thou accept?

ORSEO:
                                        I will.

MARCO:
Those words are melody unto mine ears!
I'll forthwith seek Bianca to accept
On thy behalf. If thou art mindful of 't,
I can delay the spyglass here some days.
Its brassy funnel heed as though an oracle.

[Exit MARCO]

ORSEO:
Why did I not retort refusingly?
My skills and wits evaporate as one,
Deserting cowardly when needed most.
What use is it to grip this chisel's hilt
That rusts from expectation unfulfilled?
If writer's block besets the scriveners,
This unsurmounted splinter of the Earth
Must surely be a chipper's block. And yet,
This thraldom unto blue-blood vanity
May charm anew mine inspiration's spring
To be more giving than a fount in drought.

[Enter MARIA]

MARIA:
Good day to you, young sir.

ORSEO:
                                        [Aside] Thou made it else.

MARIA:
You swore your rent would be defrayed today.

46

ORSEO:
That augury of sunny days has clouded o'er.

MARIA:
You have not paid for many moons!

ORSEO:
Alack!
Few joys I'd relish more than for my debts
To be dispelled like enemies by war,
But I can't pay! I want the wherewithal.

MARIA:
That same lament did chafe mine ears last week.

ORSEO:
And my condition has not altered since!

MARIA:
This will not do. This will not do at all!
My leniency –

ORSEO:
Ha!

MARIA:
– is ill abused.
'Tis not enough to dure thy cobbling hammering
That shods my dreams to make them flee,
Thou raze my stairs with all these heavy bricks
Thou lug up here across the sacred night,
And now thou wilt evade my rightful dues?

ORSEO:
At present, I lack th' means to pay!

MARIA:
Indeed?

47

Then I shall serve myself of value hence.
[Picks up the *Virgin*]

ORSEO:
Replace that figurine at once,
Lest thy grimy talons make its beauty wither!

MARIA:
'Tis broken, but the best of th' ordure here.

ORSEO:
What? Ordure! Thou'rt the foulest pile of that
To ever tweak my nose!

MARIA:
[Slaps him] What durst thou speak?
Scrape knees in thanks I do not hurl thee out,
But only take this statue as a bond.

ORSEO:
By all the flames of Hell, thou'lt take it not!

[They struggle over the statue. MARIA prevails when ORSEO
is again seized by a bout of coughing.]

MARIA:
'Twill grace mine hearth or else a pawnshop please.
And if thou hast not discharged this deal of debts
By th' sequent week, I'll have thee sowled before
A *gonfaloniere*'s[4] falcon eyes.

ORSEO:
Thou keepers o' quarters murmur midst thyselves
To pin thy prices high as piglet squeals
For chambers overhorrid e'en for sows!
But woe the moment of thy tenants any wretch

---

[4] A Florentine magistrate.

Behindhand but an instant lags, for thou
Descend'st on him with threats of darkest hue
To prod him with thy forking tongues to quicker ruin.

MARIA:
Thou'rt not behindhand by one instant, knave,
But many months in many instances!
Why not avail thyself of earnest work
Like stacking crates in th' port, or masonry?
It pays to lay the stone, not powder it.

ORSEO:
Stacking crates? Ha! Thou'lt be sainted sooner
Than I descend to heaving out my brains!
And laying is for pecking hens like thee!
I'm made for more than brutish drudgery!

MARIA:
I'll next bring guards in case thy manner gives them
[work.
If thou pay'st not me then, they'll turn thee out,
And all thy rubble heap on thee!

ORSEO:
Avast!

[Exit MARIA with the *Virgin*]

My work! Cantankerous old harridan!
She'll doubtless hang her washing on its arms.
O this intolerable rut that is my lot!

[Lies. Enter MARCO]

MARCO:
Orseo, I just passed thy landlady,
The *Virgin* tucked beneath her arm as though
A market goose. Didst thou vend it to her?

ORSEO:
Faith, no. She'll ransom it in lieu of rent.
I have defaulted for a trine of months.

MARCO:
That statue's worth a palatial rent –

ORSEO:
And so thou ever grind it into me,
Yet I eke out less than this hovel's cost!

MARCO:
I'll speak with her, but thou must start to scale
Thy mountainous commission, and forthwith.

ORSEO:
O let me sleep…

MARCO:
                     How, sleep? The tower-bells
Salute at midday's pomp and thou wouldst sleep?

ORSEO:
Aye.

MARCO:
                     Is thine illness gaining such a grip
That thou prostrate thyself when it commands?
[Pause]
So be 't. I shall awake thee presently.
Thou need'st to hew the silhouette ahead.
And what is this oppressive, furnaced air
That's stifling mine alertness too? I'll sit…

[Sits and droops. A pause. As his eyes are closing, enter
VIGILIA]

VIGILIA:
I seek Orseo. Is he here?
These undulating puffs betray a sinner's sleep.
I may yet cause the last of breaths in you…
[She approaches the sleeping MARCO and feels for his throat.]
'Tis here, that fragile rope of sustenance.
Atropos only needs to snip its twines
And then you're cast adrift to float away,
No longer anchored to this flesh of life.
If I am sudden, I might do the act.
Just tight my grip and crush your vileness out,
As if 'tis pus that swamps a fetid scab.
Yet would it serve me good? What would transpire?
For you would be released in but one gasp,
Mayhap out of a happy, cradling dream,
Then lauded loud at pious funeral.
But th' muck that courses in your veins would plash at
[me
Capture, torture lasting godless ages.
Your suffering would be an exhalation
While I would sigh my torments every day.
No. It will be another way. Awake,
Villain!
[Shakes him. MARCO wakes.]

VIGILIA:
I hear your sound. Speak not, but list.

MARCO:
[Whispering] Vigilia!

VIGILIA:
                        The same. No more from you.
You doubtless sought from thoughts to banish me,
And yet I'm here, a walking memory,
An entrail of that carnage past all words
You perpetrated. Now I've come with news,
And news that thunders Heaven with outrage:

51

That abhorrent seed which you did basely
And violently plant in me has taken root.
A surgeon, doubly feed for secrecy,
Confirmed the dread. Your worm is in my fruit.
Have words affrozen to your tongue? Perchance
Remorse's smoke that ever close pursues
Each fiery act's now blackening your heart,
Occasioning your eyes with tears to smart.
I hope it is, but you'll taste worse than that!
Your crime's so vile, made fouler that it was
Against my trodden being carried out.
You stole so much from me who has much less
Than any pauper lit with half an eye.
Do not expect that what you have begun
Will be completed. No. In that I intercede,
For Marco I can't bring myself to tell.
Though he is only half-uncle to me,
He stocked my days with much more love and care
Than any direct brother could provide.
If he unearthed the truth beneath the stone,
He would arraign you rightly to a duel,
With hope that that most odious of thoughts
That it was he who introducéd us
Would be sepulchred with your burial.
But for his service unto justice true
He would be thanked with dungeons' cold embrace,
Or worse, for you might kill him if his arm
Is trembling with the poisoned blood of rage.
O circularity of circumstance!
He must preservéd be from knowing it,
So death I choose both for myself
And for your Hell-blown kiss. It shall be done,
And done in such a way that you ne'er will
Its scene from your remembrance extirpate.
It will remain, your mind to madness stain.
God grant you will be inculpated too.
My death comes sudden now! Adieu!

[Rushes to the window, throws it open and exit]

MARCO:

Vigilia!

[Rushes to the window. Exit MARCO, running. ORSEO stirs upon the couch.]

ORSEO:
Methought I heard some words, yet I'm alone.
Are my phantasms clothed with powers new?

[Enter MARCO, no longer wearing his cloak. He goes to the window, looks out, then closes it.]

MARCO:
[Aside] No. She erred. I am too weak to kill him.
Yet this black cloud won't melt until it rains revenge.
Her ghost will be appeased... I swear.

ORSEO:
What are those muttered words that crouch beneath
Mine ears?

MARCO:
Dost thou recall...?

ORSEO:

What of her?

MARCO:

Ah!

She swells the tearful ranks of Purgatory.

ORSEO:
That cannot be... But said thou "Purgat'ry?"
Marco, is that to say her death was –

53

MARCO:

                                       Thought
And executed by her troubled self.

ORSEO:
This news weighs heavier than any slab
That stands within this room. How harsh it is
Of final partings never to imply
Their nature, and be only later shown
As dark impostors of normality!

MARCO:
There's more. She was some months enceinte.

ORSEO:

                                           She was?

Know'st thou the father?

MARCO:

                              Only by suspicion.

ORSEO:
Who is 't?

MARCO:
        A brute whose name won't stale my breath.

ORSEO:
How did she die?

MARCO:
                She fell, as though an autumn leaf
That has been blown by cruel storms of life
Off th' branch of Santa Trinita's old bridge,
Unheeding of its watchful Holy Three.
She fell and only Charon pulled her out.
She drowned in pain of corpus and of mind…

ORSEO:
The world's been done a service!

MARCO:
What saith thou?

ORSEO:
One who so cheaply prizes children's lives
Deserves no lordship over her own one.

MARCO:
Orseo, she –

ORSEO:
That infant could have been
The finest work of bloods' coincidence,
The heir, perchance, t' a cornucopia
Of great inventions' possibilities,
A spring of dynasties of genius!

MARCO:
And was the mother but a tool for that!?
Wasn't she perchance a "finest work" as well?
Thou... words elude me... This I can't digest!
'Tis mockery that shreds sad mourning's veil.
[Aside] If I don't leave forthwith, I'll harm us both.

[Exit MARCO]

ORSEO:
Why did she not tell me? Why throw away
A benison like mouse the cat left by the door,
Destroying two when she could have created one?
And Marco... why's his temper like a wick?
Or does the compass of his reason point
Suspicion's arrowed fingers towards me?

[Lies. Enter MARCO upon the stage balcony]

MARCO:
This vantage shows his window patently,
The eye whence she like teardrop fell... Heavens!
My bile so blackens, I could –

[Enter GUILDSMAN, hooded]

GUILDSMAN:
                              Kill him?

MARCO:
                                        What?
Who's there? Come, breathe your name and shed your
                                          [cowl!
GUILDSMAN:
I'll show you not my scowl, but only this.
[Produces dagger. MARCO draws.]

MARCO:
What are you at, and what will you with me?

GUILDSMAN:
Know you Orseo Valentini?

MARCO:
                      Sir,
I know him well. Yet why this dagger's fang?

GUILDSMAN:
The blade is meant for him. The hilt for you.
Observe, 'tis graped with precious stones.
But stone grows precious through the way 'tis cut,
And men in ambuscades will guard those ways.
[MARCO sheathes]

MARCO:
Your murky words assume lucidity –

56

GUILDSMAN:
And gold upon them glints. Take it.

MARCO:
                                        Pray, hold.
Although I comprehend... do I accept?

GUILDSMAN:
Aye! Take it! Opportunity will give it work.

MARCO:
No. No! He is a brotherly dear friend,
I cannot do it! An engagement waits,
I must be gone!

GUILDSMAN:
                        If your hand leaves this knife,
You may receive it in another part.

[Gives MARCO dagger and exit GUILDSMAN]

MARCO:
Oh God! Out of this place, and quit its thought.

[Exit. The stage darkens.]

Act III

[A room in the Cristobaldi palace. (Orseo's statues can be
hidden behind draperies for a quick scene change.) A table
stands in the middle. Enter MARCO and 3 servants, each
bearing one of Orseo's medium-sized statues, which they place
side by side upon the table. Enter BIANCA, attended.]

MARCO:
Madam, ever I remain your servant.

[Kisses her hand]

BIANCA:
What be thine offerings for us today?

MARCO:
Here grieves a *Pieta*, your ladyship.
A finely crafted sculpture, you will grant,
A psalm inscribed upon that sorrowed face.
Methought your chapel might –

BIANCA:
                                        Indeed!
'Tis praying for a *Pieta*. The present one
Is crumbling most irreverently soon.

MARCO:
Milady, this is fashioned o' finest marble
That is conceived in Italy's famed earth.
This *Pieta*'s as solid as your faith,
And everlasting as your family.

BIANCA:
I'll buy it. And this nymph?

MARCO:
                                Egeria,
Being turned into eternal fountain.
On my visit to your country villa,
(For which dear pleasure I still owe bowed thanks)
I chanced to meet an empty pediment
That lacked a mistress like a puppy lost.

BIANCA:
'Tis right. She will baptise the pool surrounds.
Now what completes your varied trinity?

MARCO:
Prometheus, reined in by torment's chains.

BIANCA:
I have already seven of his sort!
No more, or I can furnish him a shrine
And be subject to doubts of paganry.

MARCO:
Can't madam's pity be convinced t' adopt
This fallen god who's torn by elements?
Look at this tortured straining in his limbs
And features. Is 't not marvel to behold
Humanity's whole grief distilled in stone?

BIANCA:
I will not take it, that I firmly state!
Why should I pay for misery to be
A tenant in my house when I have been
Yet fortunate to halt it at my door?
Is 't not too common a commodity
Beyond these walls? And rendered in the flesh?
Methinks my money would be better spent
On blessing torment's live examples with mine alms.
Besides, this figure is too finical.

MARCO:
As madam will. Permit me now to steer
Towards the sordid matter of their price.

BIANCA:
The starting volley I will let thee shoot.

MARCO:
Two hundred florins for the pair

BIANCA:
Thou overprice thy charges like a doting nurse!

A hundred's true confession of their worth.

MARCO:
Consider, madam, th' ruthless cost of stone!
Your number leaves above it but a slit,
Too narrow for an artist's fantasy.

BIANCA:
One hundred-fifty and no more of it.

MARCO:
Yet rumour wags it that a rival's Mars
Received more medals from your hand! Methinks
One hundred-seventy and five makes truce
Between our difference.

BIANCA:
                I've said my sum.
It holds its ground alike a stalwart guard.

MARCO:
Pray, let that soldier have eight scores for victory!

BIANCA:
O very well! But mark my words, thou takest
Most rude advantage of my weariness.

MARCO:
Ducessa, I forever walk in debt
To your most gracious nature.

BIANCA:
            [To a Servant] Fetch the sum.

[Exit Servant. A pause. Enter Servant with a small case.
BIANCA unlocks it and gives several purses to MARCO.]

Torquato, stay. The rest may leave.

60

[Exeunt Servants, save one]

                                        Now, then.
When is the soonest that thou canst commence
To sculpt my daughter's likeness?

        MARCO:
                                   Until now,
I've stolen but the briefest snatches of
Your daughter's sweet-sung beauty, signora.
If I could beg to meet th' mirage I've seen,
From nigh at hand appraise visage and mien,
My crafting tools, I've troth, would verily
Catch fire from inspiration's holy spark
When lit by her angelic radiance.

        BIANCA:
Faith, I shall have her summoned here anon,
And I shall also lend the portrait that
Most justice does to her. Torquato, go.
Call Fiorentina, and that picture find.

[Exit Servant]

As for thy fee, we'll argue it each time
I visit th' forming infant at thy school
To watch the master discipline rude stone.
Divulge thy workshop's whereabouts. I'll come.

        MARCO:
Your pardon I beseech, but that recourse
Is one unpaved by possibility.

        BIANCA:
                    How?

        MARCO:
The place where my statues all metamorphose

From rock cocoons is my most private room,
As close my being's chamber as my skull.
I've never yet let any visit it
And fear, respectfully, your ladyship,
That even your exalted ducal rank
Can purchase no exception there.

BIANCA:
                              Go to!
My meant intent's to see the bust to judge
If mine approval's met.

MARCO:
                    I dread t' expose
A lady so immaculate attired,
As you are, to the dusty disarray
That's my profession's crude companion.
It strikes me as a better route by far
To bring th' resolving sculpture, furtively,
To thy palazzo for inspection's test.

BIANCA:
Ye artisans are puzzling things indeed.
The richer is thy talent's fabric weaved,
The more the knots of foibles multiply
And thicken in 't. But so be it! Send word
Of when the seasonable day arrives.
What stays my child? These servants seem to match
Their paces to a midday shadow's creep.
All glide momentously as pendulums!

[Exit BIANCA]

MARCO:
No one suspects my hands have held
More silver forks than iron chisels. His the craft,
But mine the craftiness! What is the cause
Fate's favours change like phases of the moon

In how they shine upon each individual?
For why has he received a bounty's gifts
Whilst I have been outright denied the same,
Like orb and sceptre to a second-born?
Yet I so yearned to be the sculptor to
Humanity itself, but had t' endure
A frigid morn's awaking that I lacked
That instinct, fickle and unfathomable
Which dwells in some like marrow in a bone
Whilst others hollow leaves like rotted logs,
That instinct which the name of "talent" wears.
Each day I see around me faces, forms
That I would write on granite's fadeless page,
But no. Their wonder I can't pour in phrase.
Impressions enter me and there are mired,
Trapped in mine inability's ravine.
My fingers rebel over every command
That gives my mind, producing clumsy blots
Which, with maudlin eyes, I disinherit
Before they're midway to maturity.
But he, a plunderer of innocence,
Who loathes mankind enough to banish it
Without his crowded attic, he has been
Presented with the gift, nay, duty e'en
To serve as vessel t' our ideals' nectar,
Bequeathed with skill that will outlast our age
For all posterity's bewonderment.

[Enter BIANCA and FIORENTINA]

    BIANCA:
Fiorentina, here's that visioned craftsman
Whose sculptures many of our rooms adorn.

    FIORENTINA:
O! You, sir, are the father of these forms?

MARCO:
I am, good signorina, and I plead,
Knight not thy lowly servant in address.
[Kisses her hand]
[Aside] 'Tis rare the lauding garlands' petalled words
That sonnetsmiths bedeck their subjects with
Should prove so fragrant, bright and honest! – Pray,
Forgive my yawning silence, for my faculties
Surrender of themselves before your grace.

FIORENTINA:
I am most pleased to draw a gentleman
Around the dulcet voice which until now
Spoke but through lapidarian interpreters
(And only to mine eyes, regrettably)
In tones of heroism and holiness.

BIANCA:
[To Fiorentina] My child, remember who thou art.

FIORENTINA:
[To Bianca] Soft now!

MARCO:
My undeserving faint exertions are
Too base for celebration from your lips.

FIORENTINA:
But no, for thou injustice deal thyself
If through politeness fitting praise impeach.

MARCO:
The signorina's passing generous.
With thy permissions, I shall take my leave.
[Picks up the unsold *Prometheus*]

FIORENTINA:
How, was thine art's yon paragon not bought?

64

BIANCA:
We've a surfeit of the selfsame topic.

FIORENTINA:
We've both *Prometheus* and *Sysiphus*,
Yet it's your tireless error to roll them in one,
As though two balls of clay, until
Not e'en their authors could them separate.

BIANCA:
[Aside] Yet here are two that I can separate!

FIORENTINA:
This Son of Heavens ours eclipses all,
His excellence is lustred seven times as bright.
Rather him than th' others all together!

BIANCA:
If thou desire it so, it shall be got.
Name thy rate, Signor Margoli.

MARCO:
                              Madam,
I would not dare presume to press demands
When I've already been the priceless jewel paid
That is your daughter's compliment.
Accept it as my trifling gift to one
Whose taste is so refined.

FIORENTINA:
                              Thou art most kind.

MARCO:
Ducessa, signorina, mine adieux.

[Exit MARCO]

FIORENTINA:
Caress these statues, mother, with your sight.
Do they no seem to shine like dawn's first smile
With his imagination's brilliance
And his dexterity's nobility?
'Tis awe-arousing, nay astonishing
To thus behold that vast creative force
That rests its god-like throne amongst these works.
In any man, the finest quality
Is his degree of genius. Methinks
It speaks more of the purity of the soul
And elevation of the mind than any title.

BIANCA:
Fond girl! What idle thoughts divert thy sense
To air such unconsidered words? He is
A base-born parvenu, a convert, too!
A Marc'Ettore by his name,
A *mercatore*[5] by his line. But thou,
To him compared, art clad in th' finest lace
Of rank and breeding. And what's more,
These artisans inhabit briefly lustrous worlds
That flicker both in virtue and in state.
What shines the most attracts and ends such moths.

FIORENTINA:
Does not ability absolve him from
His field-grown and not garden-cultured roots?
He's in the vanguard of the most renowned
And keenest-charging sculptors in a town
That almost yields as many statues in a year
As babes. He lodges in the better part
Of the grand Lungarno Acciaoli
Where all the wealth of Florence holds its court.
'Tis also breathed he keeps a studio,
Its walls bricked with surmises. A man who bears

---

[5] Merchant

Such moment cannot be "unsteady" tarred.

        BIANCA:
It is precisely their accomplishment
Which fluffs the peacock feathers of his kind
With self-importance false and dangerous,
That lures to ruin with a demon guile.
Success is but an ermine armour: most ornate,
Embellished with acclaim and wealth,
Yet fashion's change to riband mess it shreds,
So cease. I'll suffer no more talk of him!

        FIORENTINA:
[Aside] Where hides that studio that's kept so close?
Perchance 'tis cradled in the countryside?
[Admires statues]

        BIANCA:
[Aside] This fancy for a man below our state
Assumes a forceful gravity.
It must be stifled ere it loudens into threat!
When the finished opus is delivered,
(A certain burst for her of joyed surprise)
I'll cork all dealings with this Margoli.

[Exit BIANCA]

        FIORENTINA:
How splendorous they are! How excellent
In conception and in execution.
Here ev'ry curve conspires to please the eye,
Conveying blest tranquillity, as though
A lullaby had breathed her to this shape.
Whilst here, oppression's marring cruelty
Is raged at by a god in manacles,
His fury antithesis to the first.
Tendons knot in straining at their feckles,
And blades of teeth thrust from the hilt of flews,

As if to fright the forces that have dared
Inflict this savage usage onto him,
A struggle powerful and desperate.
Last, this image of *la Dolorosa*,
Embracing in her weary arms the wreck
That was her son, that soul had fled,
Her orbs uplifted, following its winging path…
In matter each is different, in manner joined,
Children of one father, but three mothers,
And high-born progeny, for it's my faith
That there exists an aristocracy
With heraldry where talent trims the shields
And chisels, quills and lutes provide its crests.
Perchance then he and I as equals are?
For I admit my hereto exiled thought:
I entertain a certain toy for him,
But not the flaccid daisy-love which blooms
In gilded vases that one's suitors fill,
'Tis more the oaken bond nigh siblings share:
Affinity of nature and of thought.
There is some kinship that's intuitive
Between these marble beings and myself.
How I long to be his inspiration,
To see his hands caress rough rock to semble me,
Beatrice to th' Dante of the stone,
Partaking of that rite which forms, creates
And makes the human spirit brighter blaze,
For there is something cosmic in my sex,
Of vital essence t' all the alchemies of men.
If I could map him more exactly…
And so I shall! I'll have a trustfirm guard
Seek out th' Atlantis of his studio,
Break ope its secret's seal, for it's my wish
To spy him there engaged in monumental work,
To glimpse that solemn Eucharistic act
Transubstantiating talents' labours
To matter's vessels in that muses' temple.

Act IV

Scene 1

[The studio again. ORSEO is working on the statue of
Fiorentina. Enter MARCO]

MARCO:
Good morrow. I had feared that it would be
My thankless task to raise thee from a sleep
That had not run its course to dreaming's sea.

ORSEO:
Sleep? Morpheus has drunk no wine up here
Of late.

MARCO:
          Saith thou in spite of yesterday's
Atlas-effort thou hast not yet rested?

ORSEO:
Nay. Sleep's a docile dog that comes when called,
Whilst Inspiration is a seraphim less sure,
Whose high behest I firstly serve.
She unexpected comes at some tired hour,
Alighting softly on the window-sill,
With malice choosing when I am most numbed.
Then whilst I'm coaxing slumber to mine eyes,
She with suggestions niggling chews mine ears,
And torments like a squealing child its parent would,
For I must drag myself from comfort's folds
To wait on her imperious command.
She's cruel mistress, yet munificent!

69

MARCO:
I am amazed at thy vitality!
Thou drove the hacking dragon of thy malady
Beneath thee like Saint George.

ORSEO:
What malady?
A slight chill lapped up by the midday heat.

MARCO:
The statue does progress in bounds, I see.
I have unfailing faith her ladyship
Will be superbly pleased.

ORSEO:
'Tis not her pleasure
Nor others' whence fulfilment I derive.
I raise here stairs to immortality
From slabs of marble that I've sleeked so well
That they reflect of man's vast enterprise.

MARCO:
But as thou said, all works are founded on
The stones that ancient greatness set in place.
What sculptors in thy learned esteem rejoice?

ORSEO:
In Polyclitus I am overawed
By Harmony that's as immaculate
As if 'tis sung by choirs of cherubim,
Or like the Heavenly pavane of stars,
Proportions balanced on Perfection's palm,
Simplicity that proves all else bombast.
Lysippos, though, infuses more of Man
Into depictions of divinity.
His gods and heroes breathe and glare and grieve,
And he was the first to set his sculptures
Like gemstones always in admirer's midst:

70

They beauty beam wherever they're viewed from.
Yet his proportions Polyclitus ill offend.
Just see his elephantine *Hercules*
That Rome's Farneses stable in their house!
From what I've gleaned of Pheidias, methinks
He, for a sculptor, was too much an architect,
And figures built so large they could be dwelt,
Too vast a void for genius to fill.
Then Myron's statues, though they doubtless were
Correct as surgeons in anatomy,
Seem rather common, starved of godliness,
Whilst his visages for more spirit thirst.
Praxitheles I favour most of all.
Contours as softly fresh and youthful as
The pastures of Elysium. They show
Like waxworks almost melting by his vision's torch.
The first of Argives not to waste his skill
On mortal bronze which dies and gains green-mould,
Forsaking it to sign his name instead
In marble's crystal whiteness, smooth and pure.
'Tis no surprise that bronze originals
Have all expired since Greece's Golden Age,
And left but testaments in Latin stone.
I saw such copy of Praxitheles:
His *Hermes holding Dionysus as a babe.*
Its marvel did arrest my very breath!
But let us not forget that artisan
Who's grown a longer beard than old Methuselah,
Who's nurtured masterworks in ev'ry line,
Who out of custom or humility
Baptised himself as plain "Anonymous,"
The finest maker of reliquaries
For ev'ry prodigy whose merit's name
By Time's unjustly acid was effaced.
I pray I'll be delivered from that fate!

      MARCO:
What of the sculptors of our current age?

ORSEO:
Their works are mostly strangers unto me…
Are they as good as mine?

MARCO:
Recall thee not?
I brought some here for thee to study them.

ORSEO:
'Twas evidence too thin for verdict's choice.
But thou must know them all. Have they my skill?

MARCO:
My words of laud or damn are blown in vain,
For Chronos weighs us on the truest scale.
There was though one whom I regarded high:
An artist named Ligier Richier.
I met his best when I traversed through France:
An ornamented grand mausoleum.
Its lifelike horror curdled all my blood,
Yet in the puzzling way that magnets act,
Betimes what should repel instead attracts.
A skeleton, with tattered rags of skin
Still clinging to that wreckage reft of life,
Holds in a mast-like, outstretched arm his heart
As though unto remembrance it's a torch,
Memento mori of our age and worth,
A sacrifice for all humanity,
Triumphing over th' ordinariness of Death
With superordinary epitaph.
[A pause]
Know'st thou *The Picture of a Thousand Woes*?

ORSEO:
If it's replete with heightened moments of
Intensity that rear to be returned
Through mine art's means, I'll hark with eager ears.

MARCO:
"The King of the Pyrus, (called Runix) enthuses:
He's known for his passions – a prince of the muses.
One day he demands to be made such a picture
That will be an oracle of dreams and the future.

He keeps at his palace a palette of painters
Yet this makes them dull without any remainders.
So Runix resolves he himself will be limner
The talent he glows with is more than mere glimmer.

But th' usual hues bled from berries and insects
Though fit for a bear, for magic have defects.
His quest for a rainbow at last brings fruition:
The sum of the wealth of his artisans' vision.

Their murders he orders with ruthless *proclivis*
That currency also repays their disservice.
He ver'ly draws blood from those lying in waste:
Their eyes are outgouged and then mixed to a paste.

The azure orbs render cerulean frescoes,
The greyish become oceanic blunt echoes,
The rarities verdant are meadows' citation,
The browns lend their tones to the mud of Creation.

When last all can marvel completion's concurment
Each stroke of the brushwork enlivens t' a serpent,
Each point begins hurtling with dagger-like fury:
They leave of King Runix a sight far too gory."

ORSEO:
Now may I ask to where this verbal bending tends?

MARCO:
Thou hat'st mankind most fervidly. This serves
Addition to thy litany of flaws.
What's more, methought that Pyrus ripped apart

73

By serpents woken by loud hubris makes a scene
Worth all the poetry of marble.

        ORSEO:
                              I'll think on it.
But let me first complete this Zephyr chore:
A puff to fright the dust.
[Blows on statue and begins to cough violently.]

        MARCO:
                Orseo!

        ORSEO:
                        Ah!
I have to… persevere… yet I… cannot!
[Collapses]
        Rise, rise, damned mass! Why can't this feckless flesh
Be braver servant to its master? Oh!
Marco, my soul is slow expiring out of me,
An organ-pipe's last mournful, trailing note!
I'm dying. Dying! All these lumps of sternest stone,
I have imbued them with my spirit's breath,
Until there was too little left in me.
And yet, I must urge on. *Faiblesse oblige*!
Here frowns my last and greatest masterpiece.
I shudder now to drop it incomplete,
Unhatched, to break within this captious world,
I quake to be garrotted in the midst
Of this exquisite swan-song's closing chimes.
It must have conclusion's final polish!
It has to be so absolute a crown
That even if my statues' kingdom is
All crumbled out of memory save this,
'Twill amply chronicle the wonders lost,
Astounding dedication to myself
And unto her who is this figure's twin!
This work's the chalice of my skills' rich wine
Matured through lifetime of experience!

74

I must go on! Go on! Avast, vile Death!
There's plenty others who have dried of life!
Why axe this tree that drinks yet living's dew?
O rise, thou pitiable sack of meat!
I am too great to die, too young to die!
There's so much left to do and see and know!
Why is our life, this chest wherein we hide
The blinks we steal from Time so very cramped?
Cramped like coffins with the dead… O Heaven!
I can't abide th' idea that is Death,
To be no more, to end, to disappear!
For only life and time are certainties,
Adversaries that wrangle over us.
Time always wins, victorious oblivion.
I want to, nay, deserve to live forevermore!
I want to breathe, create, and neither cease!
Instead, the hearse of sickness waits on me,
Death hammers on my door with fistful coughs.
All greatness draws the tax of suffering!
Like hound that's smelt a fault, it tracks, pursues
The swiftest minds as if it would reclaim
The superfluity that has been gifted them,
And spurs them with the snapping jaws
Of illness, indigence, or solitude
To further speed and greatness that is born
Out of that mighty battle's elements,
The phoenix that arises from the arson's ash.
But like a taper burning twice as bright,
My fate's to burn out quicker than the rest.
It is that cursing, blessing suffering
Which lets one draw a well most recondite
That holds the mercury and nectar of man's nature.
Thou, Marco, live too well to ever know 't.
That's why thy poor essays to sculpt turn out
As if a madman hewed them in the dark.
I sought salvation from it in my craft,
But that has only dredged me more of it:
The gentle powder-bark that growing carvings shed

75

Invades my lungs and ever strengthens there
A choking, deadly stranglehold. Look 'round,
I've screamed mine ache through these contorted
[mouths

And cried through those dolorous oculi.
My torment's sacrifice ennobles them,
And soon, with Christlike passion, I'll die for them!

MARCO:
[Aside] Now Son of God he styles himself. –
Reel in thy desperation. Hardship meet
With th' fortitude of Stoic hardiness.

ORSEO:
O salt me not with biting platitudes!

MARCO:
Soft now! Regain thy peace and rest.
[Helps ORSEO to the couch.]

ORSEO:
Mayhap
This cradle's false embrace my death-kiss shall
[provide…

MARCO:
Nay, steer thy thoughts to sleep's lagoon.
[ORSEO lies]
[Aside] I want the knowledge this to reconcile
With mine own shrouded course. I must away!

[Exit MARCO. As ORSEO is falling asleep, enter MARIA.
She does not see Marco. The lighting changes to show that
Orseo is seeing Maria in a nightmare.]

MARIA:
O marry! Creasing all his coverlets
When honest hands are yet in service of the day!
That's why the villain is so mean in funds.

Well then! Let's see what can be auctioned here!
[Picks up a small statue]
What am I bid for this? Two florins? Three?

[An auction is improvised with actors 'planted' in the audience.
This should involve members of the audience as well. ORSEO
meanwhile stirs in the throes of this dream. When everything has
been sold:]

And last, this slave well-ridden with disease.
A tolerable feed for hunting hounds.
What am I bid for him? One florin, less?
Who'll take away this worthless mound of rags?

[ORSEO sits up in a scream. Exit the dream-MARIA quickly.
Lighting returns to normal. ORSEO lies back. Enter MARIA,
this time real.]

MARIA:
O marry! Creasing all his coverlets
When honest hands are yet in service of the day!
That's why the villain is so mean in funds.
Up, up thou varlet!

ORSEO:
What's this shout?

MARIA:
I'm here
To harvest in thine overripened dues.

ORSEO:
There's naught to harvest in. Have pity, pray!

MARIA:
So! Thou think'st this tenement's an abbey
Where invocations lodge thee free? Out! Out,
Thou miserable, good-for-nothing cur!

These figurines now all append to me,
They'll sweep the dung-heap of the debts thou stooled,
But thou canst go thy way!

ORSEO:

Thou churlish brach!

MARIA:
Thou resty idler! I shall have thee hence!
Guards are loitering on yonder corner.
I'll pay them well to throw thee far!

ORSEO:

Begone,
Thou frumpold toad! My friend returns anon,
And he shall pay them to throw thee!

MARIA:

Will he?
Indeed? There's something that thy torpid thoughts
Should swirl around amidst their indolence.
I'm speaking of a certain maid who died.

ORSEO:
Vigilia? What knowest thou of her?

MARIA:
More than I care to share. I note her name
Has tensed thy mouth with consternation's cords...

ORSEO:
O speak, thou pestilent curmudgeon! Speak!

MARIA:
I know full well the crime thou nailed in her.
I know 't well!

ORSEO:
>What? What canst thou know, eh? What?

MARIA:
An urgent rancour summoned me unto thy door,
But whilst mine ears toiled at untangling sense
From out the chaos orgying within,
The door burst ope, and she with hurt a-flushed
And hued with desperation past me rushed.
Then when she came next time –

ORSEO:
>What "next" was there?

MARIA:
Thou lolled in customed idle slumbering,
But not thy friend (and I can scent a gentleman
Despite the reeking company he keeps!)
So she, mistaking him for thee, told all
To him.

ORSEO:
Thou keyhole-leeching, lying wretch!

MARIA:
She wished for thee to bleed some blame for it,
That's why she out thy window dashed herself.

ORSEO:
Thou liest, fell witch! She in the Arno drowned,
And Marco told me so!

MARIA:
>He was the first
To reach her corpse and cede his coat as shroud.

ORSEO:
I do recall some noise that roused me then...
He lacked a cape as well. And midst his temples
A grave distraction made its raven perch.
This tale embraces all those orphan facts...

MARIA:
So when the guards arrive for thine arrest,
I but need to tickle recollection
To make him less forgiving than he's been.
I've glinted threat at thee. Make not me use its blade!

ORSEO:
My God! If Marco knows... And even more
Disquieting: he's never broached his doubt,
A cemeterial deep silence.
What means that minatory gentleness?

MARIA:
Now that truth and thee are well acquainted
Why not begin to stuff thy sack to go?
And never scrape my threshold's step again!

ORSEO:
I've told thee, I shall not go hence!

MARIA:
                                        O! O!
Then stay! 'Tis simpler game to capture thee.
Yet ere I go to fetch the law's brave agents,
I shall begin removing hence thy wares.
[Picks up a *Cupid*]

ORSEO:
A cupid for thy loved cupidity,
How pelting modest.

MARIA:
                    I shall take this first.
Th' one I sold was feathered with ten florins.
He might be finer bird!

ORSEO:
                    Ten florins? Fie!
They've never earned so much. Thou liest again!

MARIA:
And thou or art or play a fool
To walk in twilight of their value.

ORSEO:
                              Put it down.

MARIA:
Start lading, miscreant!

ORSEO:
                    Out of my rooms!

MARIA:
Out thyself! And thy rooms? Ha!

ORSEO:
                         Give me that statue!

MARIA:
Thine ev'ry straw of hope is reaped!
The law, thy friend, and I: three busy serfs
Whose iron forks are antlered with thy dues,
Thine idleness and thy gross deeds. We three
Condemn thee now to lose thy home, chattels,
And liberty.

ORSEO:
          No! Paint me not that Hell!

My blood is richer fluid than mortal muck!
There's nothing that can dam its conq'ring course!
No! Nothing! Nothing!

[They struggle]

MARIA:
Murder!

ORSEO:
Have at thee!
[Hits her on the head with the statue. MARIA faints.]
That will lodge a lesson in thy noddle!
Now what am I to do with this old crab
Before it finds its quick anew? By Mars,
I have it! She will be most pleasantly mewed up!

[The stage darkens.]

Scene 2

[The following day. A new, full-sized statue fills the room, its
eyes turned heavenwards, its pose devout. Enter MARCO]

MARCO:
How, up at cockshout?

ORSEO:
Even earlier.

MARCO:
Orseo, whence this figure, here so suddenly?
And plaster's butter, too? I had supposed
That thy devotion unto marble was
Religious past all change!

ORSEO:
I fickle proved.

I found a vat of it, concealed from even me,
And thought it right to give employment to 't.
Now I intend to pour a yolk of bronze
Around its shell. Know'st thou a foundryman
Who's rich in skill, yet pauperish in cost?

MARCO:
I'll seek one out, though my bewilderment
Still numbs my thoughts.
[Noises off]

ORSEO:
                              What is that troop without?
We seem about to host some visitors!
[MARCO examines the statue]

MARCO:
This plasterwork –

[Enter a CAPTAIN and Two Guards]

CAPTAIN:
                              Signor Margoli! You're found here?
[Aside] This will delight a certain lady's ears. –

MARCO:
Whence know'st thou me?

CAPTAIN:
                              Your fame precedes you, sir
Which of you gentlemen is lodger of
These rooms?

ORSEO:
            I am.

CAPTAIN:
                              [Aside] Margoli's hiding it! –
83

We seek Maria Vindice, the owner here.

ORSEO:
You do? What is her crime? Or have you found
A cure for all-consuming greed, perchance?

CAPTAIN:
She quit her place and –

The Statue:
                              Murder.

CAPTAIN:
                              Did you speak?

ORSEO:
Not I.

CAPTAIN:
        I heard the name of "murder" muttered low.
Signor Margoli, did you say it?

MARCO:
                              No.

CAPTAIN:
Did nothing scrape your ears?

ORSEO:
                              No. Not a squeak.
Unless the window's mouth was whence it came.
Mayhap you're called for in the street below.

CAPTAIN:
I would have waged my honour and my life
That it was here pronounced.

ORSEO:
                              You err, good knight.
Methinks old battles echo in your head!

CAPTAIN:
Most odd. [To Guards] Didst thou two fellows nothing
                                        [catch?
[To Orseo] Can you embroider us with no detail
Of where your landlady has vanished to?

ORSEO:
I know not, sir.

CAPTAIN:
                      Good day then, gentlemen.
Our pardon for th' intrusion's gracelessness.

[Exeunt the CAPTAIN and Guards]

MARCO:
It spoke, Orseo! Aye, the statue spoke!

ORSEO:
Thou hast the Captain's cat-like audience,
Or else his peacock-feathered fantasy,
For I heard naught.

MARCO:
                      The statue spoke, I swear!
And this Maria, too. Where has she gone?
Both odd, as if this building is bewitched.

ORSEO:
Good riddance of that vile, Medusa-hag!
The building's rather de-witched with her gone.
[MARCO examines the statue again]

MARCO:
On this statue. Where… Good grief, Orseo!
I've just received a thunderbolting thought!
Is this…?

ORSEO:
    Thou hast anatomised it with
Commendably sharp cunning, for, within,
My well-defunct tormentor is interred.

MARCO:
Then thou hast done a most atrocious crime!
The law's ministers –

ORSEO:
                Noted naught amiss in it.

MARCO:
They heard the statue's accusation –

ORSEO:
                          Ha!

MARCO:
And they've recorded her as disappeared!

ORSEO:
And I say, let 'em record it thousand times!
They'll scarce arrive at looking into there!

MARCO:
But thou hast killed her!

ORSEO:
                I did no such thing!
I cuffed her on the dome with Cupid, and,
When she awoke, her eggish eyes
Could wondering admire the cake I baked her in.

She got the lot of th' salted spouse of Lot!
A dress of just redress!

MARCO:

A fearful fate!

ORSEO:
Thou hold'st she did not merit it? See here!
Look at her now, more perfect thus in death
Than ever in her croaking, avaricious life.
Mine art has made her better than she was.
She lifts a pious gaze to God and sends,
Along a sunbeam, prayer that her sins
And claw-extracted wealth forgiveness gain.

MARCO:
Canst thy sins gain forgiveness too?

ORSEO:
I've cut no wound that pardon's balsam needs:
My act was apt! This wretched creature dared
To interpose her insignificance
Between mine Apollonic genius
And th' oracle through which it speaks: my craft.
The witch had uttered rapine threats that she
Would fling my children in a pawnshop's cauldron
To boil off them the value of their skin.
I could not stand such outrage spewed at me!
I was entitled t' rid the world of her
By my superiority's divinest right!

MARCO:
[Aside] O how he frolics in his devilry! –
Thou frightest me, Orseo. Thou art like
A ciphered book where all the letters mix,
For when I've solved a loud encomium,
Thou turn'st the page and it is scribbled full
With riddled words of darkest sorcery.

And this… this is too ghoulish to describe!

ORSEO:
Then cart it quickly to a foundry for
Cremation mid the flames of Hell itself.

MARCO:
I'll send those porters who the marble brought.

[Enter a Messenger]

For me?

[Takes letter. Exit Messenger. MARCO reads.]

[Aside] Bianca Cristobaldi's hither bound
With steps of dignified advance. Methinks
That Captain who knew me draws pay from her.
I must be swift and politic, or else
The lid that scheming fitted will burst off
This velvet-trimmed Pandora's box
That I have fashioned with Orseo's unnamed aid.

ORSEO:
What is yon sheet?

MARCO:
A sail to fleet me hence
Upon most eager business. Adieu!

[Exit MARCO]

ORSEO:
He's right, and lends my vexing conscience voice.
An execrable deed that worst damnation meeds.
Now two have I uprooted from this world,
And what have I supplanted their loss with?
These hollow echoes, shadows, whiffs of life,

That forest-maze of action, sense and thought?
[Kneels before the statue of Vigilia]
> Forgive me, goddess who art fair.
> Lay mercy's hand upon my sinning head.
> I'm but a man, of clay and marble ill composed.
> Tell me, why is it that the revelry
> Of Dionysiac destruction always throbs
> With more seductive, louder beat than does
> The higher, Apollonic hymn that sings
> Creation's joy? What took a thousand hours
> Being nurtured, sleeked and ornamented
> Can shattered be to powder in a blink.
> One's darkest lust, the other godly love,
> Yet both fill out an emptiness in man,
> And like unfriendly liquids battle in his mind,
> O raging, maddening duality!

[Enter MARCO]

MARCO:
> My friend, I'm direct from an apothecary.
> By tireless imploration he's agreed
> To see thee for a negligible fee,
> Which I'll discharge. Thy pale condition's ghost
> Is wailing for an audience with him.

ORSEO:
> How, thou wouldst me deliver to the fangs
> O' those rodent fools in capes? Nay, those who kill
> From imbecility and not out of
> Some provocation are a baser breed
> Than anything that sewers foul infests!
> I'll sip no nostrum cures, rank gatherings
> Of odours poisonous to all that thinks!
> Nor will I let them tap my veins and purse!
> If I had wish for blades to enter me
> I could me square a fight with ruffians,
> Who would not charge for privilege so base.

I spurn all medics and their remedies!
[Lies]

       MARCO:
This one's a man of truer quality.
Upon his coat-hook I've hung sundry plaints
O'er many years, which he has either healed
As fast as saintly touch, or else confessed
The ills not even Galen could have solved.
There must a physic be to rein thy moods!

       ORSEO:
Thou wouldst this Tempest of Creation reined?
Be off with thee!

       MARCO:
            O force thyself to see
This serves thy benefit!

       ORSEO:
              I wish t' repose.

       MARCO:
And I, I wish to save thee! Dost thou not recall
Thy genuflecting desperation's cries?
Thine ailment daily darkens in its hue.
It robs thee of thy nature! Even now
Thy melancholy stays thine hands from work
And binds thee to a couch of pouting weariness.
At other times, thy vigour overflows
To acts that later sober to remorse.
'Tis that vicissitude that I would rein,
To make thine humours less a pendulum.

       ORSEO:
Thou dost not know it all. My tempers rule
The sleep and waking of my genius,
They are my mental chiaroscuro's tempera.

MARCO:
What of the pursy husk within thy throat,
That comes as sure as winter's rattling winds?

ORSEO:
Oh leave me be!

MARCO:
     Why acquiesce thou not
To call upon the doctor if thine hours
Are whiled in incapacity's slow crawl?
Thou wouldst put faster saddle on thy time!

ORSEO:
No!

MARCO:
  I have certain troth his stratagems
Can overwhelm some regiments at least
Of that vast force of aches besieging thee.
Orseo, if thou dost not kneel thyself
By th' altar of wise Aesculapius,
Then Pluto'll strike thee off thy feet instead!
Didst thou not fret thyself to slivers at
The dread to leave this sculpture half-complete,
An orphaned infant doomed to ne'er mature?

ORSEO:
Go out... to brave oppressive voids?

MARCO:
        A prince
Is poorer in caprices than thou art!
'Tis close to hand as any elbow is,
And thou canst choose the near embrace of walls
If wide piazzas seem to swallow thee.

ORSEO:
No, Marco. I cannot.

MARCO:
Why? What checks thee?

ORSEO:
People! Shouting, jostling, stinking, crushing,
A mangle for the soul!

MARCO:
A company
Of players works the city furthest reach.
Their execution of Melpomene's best
Has drawn all idlers like a hanging would.
The streets are drained like rivers drunk by drought.

ORSEO:
No, no, no! Doctors, strangers, yawning skies
By clouds unmuzzled – a horrors' surfeit's there!

MARCO:
Orseo!

ORSEO:
No! I will not go!

MARCO:
[Aside] Madame de Cristobaldi is so close
Her perfume has already here arrived! –
I've rare recourse to words so poignant,
But as thou prize my friendship and ministering
In vending all thy works, take my advice!
[A pause]

ORSEO:
Reluctantly I acquiesce.

MARCO:
                              Brave words!
The shop is off the second alley left.
The caduceus signals from afar.
And now, dispatch! Remember, cite my name!

[Exit ORSEO. MARCO looks out the window. He begins to
sweep and tidy, then again looks out the window. He puts on
Orseo's apron, picks up the chisel and the mallet, and takes up a
position beside Fiorentina's almost ready bust. Enter BIANCA]

BIANCA:
Surprise has ambushed both of us.

MARCO:
                                        Indeed,
Good lady, your arrival's shot my words from me!

BIANCA:
And mine, this rookery too mean to roost.
What's more, thy housekeeper is passing rude,
Too saucy even for a galley cook.

MARCO:
I must apologise on her behalf.
She lost her mother recently to –

The Statue:
                                        Murder.

BIANCA:
                                        What?

MARCO:
[Aside] It spoke again! – What is the "what" you ask?

BIANCA:
Thou saith there's been a murder?

93

MARCO:

                                      No, in faith!
[Aside] What if evasion spurs its fluency? –
I said, her "mother."

BIANCA:

                            What has befallen her?

MARCO:

I'm loth to trouble you with servants' coils!
As for this garret, I can say this house
Doffs not its hat to wild disturbances.
Beneath it, my mind too can toil in peace.

BIANCA:

Thine other chambers, which I chanced to view
When offered that grand composition, are
As markedly dissimilar to this
As Athens is to Sparta. That's ornate
With fashion's furnishings and tapestries
But lacking forceful figures, whilst up here,
The stone is worked to its athletic peak.

MARCO:

Your ladyship must understand my need
T' avoid that any bridge be thrown between
Mine ordered West and mine aesthetic East.
They draw their sustenance from distinct suns.
One's ordinary life, the other's passion called,
And one shows not the latter publicly.

BIANCA:

Are those instruments but for thy digits
To creep upon like ivy?

MARCO:

                      No, indeed!
[Makes a few uncertain chips near the bust's base]

94

A further reason for concealment advocates:
The secrecy of isolation is
One of my vitalmost materials.
My sharpened mind full peace requires to sew
Its woven thoughts with deft and careful moves
Upon the marble's fabric.

       BIANCA:
                         Very well.
I'll run my business on short a leash.
The likeness is progressing pleasingly,
And wins mine admiration. I shall pay
Two hundred fifty florins roundly, less
If thou proceed to chaffer like a fishmonger.
When thy commission at its finish docks
Thou shalt not call at out palazzo, nor
Accost us over any matter. That command
Is sealed with pain of gravest consequence.
Send word when done, and I shall have it ta'en.

       MARCO:
But Madam, why?

       BIANCA:
                   Methinks thine artful orbs
Have seen enough of th' anamorphoses
In my daughter's nature to paint answers.

       MARCO:
Your daughter?

       BIANCA:
                Mine instructions I've pronounced.
I trust thou undertakest to adhere to them
As moss unto our dungeons' ancient walls.

       MARCO:
Your dignity and riddles match a sphinx!

Though I am puzzled by your words no end,
Signora bids, and I comply.

BIANCA:
                    'Tis well.
I shall now take my leave.

MARCO:
                    If I may be
So bold as beg your ladyship most kind,
In light of prior rallied reasons' force,
To not divulge the disposition of this place
And graciously indulge to honour me
With sequent visits at my proper residence –

BIANCA:
There will not any sequent visit be
On my behalf, and nor on thine I trust.

MARCO:
But naturally, madam.

[Exit BIANCA]

                    And adieu!
[MARCO takes off the apron and downs the tools]
          What's cleft this chasm betwixt us, whence this chill
                                        [now blows?
          And th' mention of her daughter, too?
          I barely dare to coast the blissful thought
          That Fiorentina de Cristobaldi's lips
          Have voiced affection towards me!
          My longing, wand'ring hope has refuge found
          In th' venerable temple of her heart…

[Enter ORSEO]

ORSEO:
What was that stately drapery that swept past me
Upon the stairs? She seemed to exit hence.
And speaking o' sweeping, why is ev'rything
As spotless as a young nun's conscience here?
Hast thou assumed the aproned office of
Minister of the bucket and the broom?

MARCO:
No, but methought it better for thine health
If thou dwell'st not Aegean stables' filth.

ORSEO:
But who was that grand dame? A buyer?

MARCO:
                                                    No.
No, she... she wished to take advantage of
The prospect through thy window's glance. Most odd!

ORSEO:
I trust thou mad'st her pay for that conceit!

MARCO:
Faith, she parted half a florin thinner.
[Gives ORSEO money]
            But pray, tell all! What did the medic speak?

ORSEO:
More Latin than old Cicero! He gave
A potion claimed to be of benefice
Against untimely sleep... but not untimely death.

MARCO:
Thou'lt not revert to such ill-boding thoughts!

ORSEO:
His help was precious small, but to forsake

97

This chessboard-square for th' gentle breeze of change
Blew cobwebs off my dusty fantasy.
I'll set my tools a merry jig again!

MARCO:
For that I am relieved. I'll grant thee peace.

[Exit MARCO. The stage darkens.]

Act V

[Later the same day. ORSEO sleeps upon the couch.
Fiorentina's bust seems all but finished. Enter FIORENTINA
and the CAPTAIN]

FIORENTINA:
Soft! Art thou certain that he's gone?

CAPTAIN:
                                    I saw him leave.
But Signorina, pray, wait not for him.
Your mother, the Lady Cristobaldi,
Hath charged me that you are expressly banned
From coming hither, or receiving him.

FIORENTINA:
Then thy disservice to my mother is
An equal to thy service unto me.
The estimation of my family
Thou hast nor gained nor lost, and may so leave.
[Gives him money]

CAPTAIN:
I do enjoin you –

FIORENTINA:
Go!

[Exit the CAPTAIN]

My heart courants
As I ingress this hallowed shrine wherein
He wrestles petrous Titans, taming them
From savagery to heroes, demigods
And nymphs forlorn. But hold, what's here?
This centrepiece all others circle like
A gloria? It seems... and yes, it is!
A skilled and faithful copy of my face!
But how did he arrive at piecing it
From th' fragments of one meeting broken soon?
I must have been engraved upon his note
With strong affection's constant points.
And what a just depiction! It's as if
I've exeated my corpus and observe it through
A distant mirror's clouded glass.
Creation of such rich vividity
Usurps magnificence from God himself,
A skill to make, beget, conceive, invent
Articles more fixed than screaming offspring.
That is the satined carpet leading Man
From midst a pack of animals towards
The throne of lordship over them. I hold
That art's vocation is the vanquishment
Of all our human failings: spiteful greed,
And beastly lust and clay-like weaknesses,
And as the last and fiercest t' overcome,
The monster of mortality itself,
Generation which proceeds beyond our juices
As glowing manifestance of our soul!
And I, a woman, can this power wield,
To channel, summon it like genie from a lamp,
For I have found the choicest exemplar
(As though it were one of his statues here)

99

Of Man, Creator: charming, elegant,
But comely too, and prosperous.
I'm not the only brook where flows our blood.
I'll let my cousins tide the dynasty
Into the future's sea. I turn my back,
Whatever's said, on that inheritance,
To court his talents' high nobility.

ORSEO:
Of whom speak you, fair signorina?

FIORENTINA:
O!
Whose voice invades my private musings here?

ORSEO:
You are the peerless Fiorentina, aye,
From the noble house of Cristobaldi,
And I know every proportion of
Your face with more precision than my name.
How comes your most poetic being hither,
To this prosaic den?

FIORENTINA:
[Aside] Disturbed and recognised!
Who is this stranger from the shadows yawned
Who challenges my secret presence here,
Like raven guarding an enchanted wood?
Some servant acolyte? – Who are you, sir?

ORSEO:
Orseo Valentini di Manieri.

FIORENTINA:
You aid Signor Margoli in his work?

ORSEO:
You err, I'm no one's servant save mine art's!

Nay, Signorina. It is more th' obverse.
The florin's tail you for its head mistook.
'Tis he who is assistant unto me,
Although he trims but prices, I the stone.

FIORENTINA:
How, you're a sculptor?

ORSEO:
Prince amongst them.

FIORENTINA:
No...
You are the miner of these marble diamonds?

ORSEO:
I proudly am.

FIORENTINA:
Then do two works completed fresh,
Prometheus and *Pieta*,
As their originator honour you?

ORSEO:
I am the father of those wayward children.

FIORENTINA:
I disbelieve you, sir!

ORSEO:
I'll show you then!
Stand hither by this open window's font
So that the golden syrup of the sun
May bathe your locks.
[Begins to carve the hair on the bust's head]
'Tis easier to sew
A sail from gentle wings of butterflies
Than to return the delicate detail

Of ev'ry wispy strand.

FIORENTINA:
You spoke the truth! You are these idols' priest!
[Aside] And how that verity revolts against
The image that my wistful fancy limned. –
This baffles all the wonders life has sprung on me,
For if you are…

ORSEO:
Why is it that
Mine authorship's uneath approved to you?
Why doubt my stature as a statuer?

FIORENTINA:
Your question marks me messenger of tidings
I would sooner swallow than deliver:
You are the victim of vile knavery.

ORSEO:
How so?

FIORENTINA:
I know not your relation's terms,
Save that this Marc'Ettore's widely claimed
That he begot this statuary.

ORSEO:
What!
You jest, good signorina.

FIORENTINA:
No, alack.

ORSEO:
I cannot credit it, for he's become
A brother's mindful substitute.

FIORENTINA:
                              It was
But yesterday my mother purchased works from him
That went by that same colour.

ORSEO:
                              Claimed as his,
You say?

FIORENTINA:
How could he feign with such audacity,
Beyond your know or censure?

ORSEO:
                              Trifling light:
I seldom venture out this cavern's womb.

FIORENTINA:
The squalid grime upon its walls writes plain
That he has starved you of your dues.

ORSEO:
                              By God!
That reason rises like a monster from the deep!
He gave me but half-florin ev'ry month,
And I, a hide bled dry, repaid with thanks
For th' agency.

FIORENTINA:
                  What? We alone him feed
Some seven hundred florins, if not more!

ORSEO:
Seven hundred? Seven hundred was their worth?
And I have sucked on but a crumb o' that feast?
And I was damned to victual myself
From th' witching kitchen of disease? O fie!
Th' injustice!

FIORENTINA:
            [Aside] This is not a man picked out
By God-hand for apotheotic rise
Upon a cloud that's wafted by the song
Of angel choirs! No, illness wrests him prone
Whilst hunger crumples him like paper in a flame.

[Enter MARCO]

            ORSEO:
Thou! Thou...

            MARCO:
            Signorina Cristobaldi!

            ORSEO:
Now is the world tipped on its head! Now is
All Heaven's canopy ripped at its seams!
Let fools at sages play and princes beg!
Let sculptures made of dung fill treasuries
And paintings done from stale line galleries,
For such a creeping trickster wormed his way
Into this cherished orchard of my fruits!
Let Hell's deep furnace vomit flames at him!
Let ramage thunderbolts dissect his limbs!
O phraseless foxship! Feigner of my name!

            FIORENTINA:
Thou'rt indebted with an explanation,
Margoli.

            MARCO:
            How? For what appeal?

            FIORENTINA:
                        Thou hast
This man most infamously ill abused
By thieving him of just acclaim and wealth,

And through the latter, also of his health.

ORSEO:
Thou Janus-headed fiend!

MARCO:
                          Pray, hold! Thou hast
Both fallen down the mineshaft of mistake.
Orseo, I am more adept than thee
In reading peoples' humours, thus I undertook
A harmless masquerade which merely aimed
To satisfy thy noble buyers' wish
To paint a face on fame, and so permit
A meeting with the artist in the flesh.
Thy late expulsion from the Guild approved my course.

ORSEO:
Now speaks the mouth whence drips the pus of lies!
Thou rig'st, base rogue!

FIORENTINA:
                        I, too, discredit it.

MARCO:
Whence this design to counter all I say?

FIORENTINA:
The one design that's here bewrayed's the plot
That thou hast spun, a spider's secret web,
Yet be assured that consequence will tighten it
Into a noose.

MARCO:
                    This goes beyond belief!

ORSEO:
Beware, O Damon, when that Pythias
Into a python pitiless transmutes!

Why, Marco, why this enmity which wore
So long the smiling mask of amity?
How long am I unwittingly enmeshed
Within this lattice built of artifice?

MARCO:
The answer in thy question hides. Thou ask
What imperfection can there dwell in thee?
Thy bloated arrogance conceals them all
Away from conscience. Creativity
Resides in great compassion or great egotism,
And thine inhabited the latter hall.
O if I had but the merest pinch, a scratch
Out of thy star-engendered talent, ah!
Thou hast no vague conception what it means
To desire ability, have ev'rything
At ready to receive it, then, alack!
Discover like the mother who a stillborn yields
That it is all denied, and worse,
To hear thou jeer my "poor essays to sculpt,"
Through tears see magnified th' iniquity
Permitting thou to squander thine to dogs
Making meretricious, pagan idols,
When thou couldst have applied that selfsame skill
To eulogise man's earthly pains and coils,
The noble sufferings of humble men,
T' inscribe a tragedy upon the brow
Of ev'ry harrowed, honest face, but no;
'Twas evanescent outward beauty that thou made
Thy tritest stock-in-trade. Thou sulked up here,
Hence shunning, loathing all mankind, for thou
Dost dare presume thyself exceptional.
'Twas that rare reptile of thine haughtiness
Which did at once repel and fascinate me –

ORSEO:
Enough!

106

[They fight. In the struggle, they knock down the plaster figure, which falls and breaks open to reveal the dead MARIA.]

FIORENTINA:
What demon bounds from out this casque?

MARCO:
The finest witness, one who can't be bribed,
Nor threatened, and whose eyes, unhued by life,
Read loud indictment unto Heaven's court!
He plucked his luckless landlady from life,
He murdered her, then thick around himself
The incense of self-righteous hubris smoked,
Maintaining through it that creating one
Bestows a licence others to destroy.
He confused his statues with our statutes,
And immortality with immorality,
The pharaoh-conceit that lording stone
Grants lordship over life!

FIORENTINA:
What tale is this
Where ev'ry scene is curtained by a fresher ghost?

MARCO:
Mark too that I said "others," pray.
This sorry hag was not the only one
For whom Orseo carved sarcophagi.
When I embarked on pirating his craft,
The rocks of moral doubt pierced hard my keel.
But then he dared to perpetrate a deed
Which in its horror justified, nay, more
Surpasséd anything I'd lanced him with,
For he, with lewd and codding luxury
Did constuprate my wretched, blind half-niece,
Vigilia, entrusted to my care
With promise that her mother's last sigh sealed.
Poor maid! Aggrieved beyond all prayers' balm

At such low usage, tainted with his sin
And robbed of dignity, alack, she chose
To pour her life-breath and his horrid seed
As from a bitter cup that's overfilled,
Through that same window that's admitting now
Th' accusing sunbeam finger of the Lord.
That, good signorina, is mine oration
Of his impeachment, that is why I own
And much rejoice in what I did, and that
Fed on my viper's nest of hate for him.

    ORSEO:
She chose to die. 'Twas mercifully quick release
From out this fleshen trap, but thou,
Thou powdered me into decrepitude
With the painful slowness of a millstone.

    MARCO:
No. Thy protracted fall is punishment
For thine excess of crimes and faults.

    ORSEO:

                          My fall?
But I will never fall. Though body will
Depart this agony and leave behind
A paltry feed for jellied maggots' maws,
My factful passing is too distant yet,
If it is to ever dawn. Those dewdrops
O' my spirit that these sculptures have upsoaked
Become eternal with them, frozen into them
Like humble flies in amber's honey snared,
The which their presence renders priced like gold.
Those legends that I fixed in solid marble
Have been profound, unfading mirrors of
Life's truest nature since the days of yore,
And their inheritance shall e'er persist
To grieve or rouse us bands of centuries ahead.
So will my statues also stand,

Still mourning my demise as monuments
To my superb, unearthly genius,
And learned men and those of taste will awe
At their divinity, and set them in
Arcades of fanciful hypotheses
Of what inspired me t' undertake that god,
Or what I thought when I infused those eyes
With wrenching misery, or whence my skill
And instinct that a mantle's folds could drape
With such precise yet natural cascade.
Those yet unborn who will remember me
Will do so for the canon I bequeathed,
And not my sins, interred with mortal meat.
But thee they'll curse a thieving epigon,
Whose name the years have digested all
Yet whose abomined being lingers like a belch
As th' one who stole a glint to bask in it
And doing so extinguishéd the brand
That was my brilliance; snuffed out the torch
That could have burnt clean through the detritus
Of autumned, grey ideas; doused the light
Ere it illuminated this base age.
I'll live till aeon's moss o'ercreeps my last known work!
My life has been achievements' march,
The promise of an immortality
That even thou couldst not expropriate.
Bright Zephyr will my gilt gondola speed
As I along Mnemosyne do float,
For even if it flows into the Styx,
Thou wilt only drown into Lethe.

    MARCO:
Not if I kill thee first.
[Picks up a chisel]
                Expel ye both
From life with but one kestrel swoop.

FIORENTINA:

Kill us?

ORSEO:
Thou want the will for it.

MARCO:

Do I? Indeed?
I could present thee as my serving-man,
Who first became unhinged from reason's jamb,
This old virago cross Hell's threshold sent,
[Points at MARIA's body]
Then weaved a wreath out of the fairest bloom
That the tree of Cristobaldi flowered.
A story to be scorned with rumour's toothless mouth,
But that I'll bear, like pecking finches are
Upon the lion's regal back. I'll do 't!
What's more, I've been commissioned by the Guild
To chisel thee from out of life – with this!
[Produces dagger]

FIORENTINA:
[aside] His truest colour's now bewrayed! To think
I worshipped such a scheming falsity
That's come to murderously peril me,
And inks the Devil's tail to write his threats.

ORSEO:
Thou cannot murder us, for that would need
A thicker lie than what thou spun so far.
Thou'lt trip on it, become thyself unhinged.
Thou canst not put thy practice into fact!

MARCO:
By Jupiter, I can't! I cannot kill,
For I am not thy breed of Daedalus
Who's lost within self-aggrandising clouds!
Yet there is something I have all the strength

110

And drive to do.
[Picks up the bust of Fiorentina and holds it high]
                         I'll shatter both of ye
Into the rubble of obscurity.

                  ORSEO:
No! Put it down!
[Tries to take it from him, but is thrown to the floor]

                  FIORENTINA:
                         Stay! Don't deepen more
Thy groove of crimes.

[Enter the CAPTAIN and Guards]

                  CAPTAIN:
                         Milady, sirs;
A volley o' voices was alarum for our ears!

                  FIORENTINA:
Thou com'st in season, Captain. Bid thy men
To wrest that sculpture from his callous hands!
My mother has already purchased it.

                  ORSEO:
He poisoned me!

                  CAPTAIN:
                         What? Poisoned, sir? That is
An allegation to be plashed with care.
[Sees MARIA's corpse]
                         And, ho! What's here? Wite to his further crimes?

                  MARCO:
'Tis not! 'Twas he, Orseo, murdered her!
And I have poisoned nobody!

FIORENTINA:
> But yes,
For what thou didst is tantamount to that.
Take him.

MARCO:
> What? Am I sentenced by a metaphor?

FIORENTINA:
Remove him!

[Exeunt the CAPTAIN and MARCO, guarded]

ORSEO:
> Left to mop betrayal's dust
With th' rags of tattered pride and sundered health...

FIORENTINA:
For all his crimes, for all his agonies,
For all his brilliance and ignorance,
I feel naught for him but some gentle pity,
Not th' awe and admiration that me lit
When I walked within the falsing shine
Of that Margoli's gross duplicity.
For then, what reason must distil from this
Is that I loved a man for bearing, looks,
The banal, common love that thousands feel.
I told myself a glib, ennobling lie
That my disowning of my birth and rank
Was for Creation's force divine, but no,
I am too shallow to be touched and stirred
By something so profound. I'm like the rest...
No cunning herbalist can succour him,
Poor devil!

[Enter BIANCA and the CAPTAIN]

> Mother!

112

BIANCA:

                  Aye, 'tis I. Speak naught,
The Captain told me of the whole intrigue.
It seems this carver's long abjured his rent.
I paid the house's ignorant new heir
To purchase all the contents of this room,
And thus discharge the debt.

        FIORENTINA:

                  What of the man?

        BIANCA:

                      What man?

[Exit FIORENTINA, crying, followed by the CAPTAIN and
BIANCA. ORSEO crawls across the stage.]

        ORSEO:
Immortality, I lived for you…

[Curtain]

Finis

113

VOYAGE WITHOUT CHARTS

Tragedy in 5 Acts

DRAMATIS PERSONAE

Lord BEAUMONT, also called KAIMI
LANI, his daughter
MANOA, a young warrior
The KAHUNA, a priest
KALANIOPU, King of Hawaii
KEAHE, his wife
NOHEA, a young woman
Two OLD WOMEN

JAMES COOK, Captain of the *Resolution*
CHARLES CLERKE, Captain of the *Discovery*
WILLIAM BLIGH   } Naval
GEORGE VANCOUVER   } Officers
JAMES KING, ship's carpenter
PHILLIPS, cabin boy of the *Resolution*

JAVEED, a pirate
Two PIRATES

Chiefs, Hawaiians, Children, Crews of the *Resolution* and the
Discovery

Act I

Scene 1

[SFX: splash of waves, straining rigging, creaking wood.]

Voice off:
Land ahoy! To starboard!

[Enter Captains COOK and CLERKE on the stage balcony, the bridge of the *Resolution*. CLERKE carries a brass telescope.]

COOK:
Quick! The telescope!
[Scans the audience]
The Sandwich Islands. Our approach from th' East
Has given them a fresher aspect.
I almost doubted them from this new view.
So widely scattered it's as if they are
By God's own hand into the ocean sown
Like seeds.

CLERKE:
They glide upon the blue with grace.

COOK:
But will we be received with equal grace,
Or like Odysseus when he returned
A second time to high Aeolia?

CLERKE:
Indeed, our parting was… inelegant.
They were at first so well disposed to us,
Accorded you the loftiest esteem,
But then, with summer storm's precipitance,
Their manner turned to coldness, then dislike,

117

Until they wished us gone most candidly.
I wonder whence that puzzling change of hue.

COOK:
The priestcraft wanted us to leave.

CLERKE:

Did they?

COOK:
The people took us for some pagan gods,
And who needs preachers where immortals walk?
We cast a shade where they had shone before,
So they did all to thrash the common sentiment
Into hostility to send us off.

CLERKE:
Good grief, is there no spot on Earth that's pure?
Perhaps I spent too little time ashore,
For I smelt not these fetid politics.

COOK:
This island's large enough for everyone.
We'll drop our anchors in another place,
And if we are disturbed, we'll move again.
There's seven islets almost in a row.
That's why upon our prior voyage here
I named the first as 'Sentinel', while that
[Points]
A Spaniard of old 'Isla Redondo' called
Which follows rightly from its flawless shape.
They cannot all be ridden with unfriendliness!
Yet I myself am troubled to return.
This infelicitously broken mast
Has levered us into a cheerless state.

[Enter BLIGH and JAMES KING]

CLERKE:
Here comes our carpenter.

COOK:
Ah, Mr King,
How long will 't take to execute repairs?

KING:
A week will be enough, sir.

COOK:
Mr Bligh,
We need a bountiful supply of fruit,
To keep far scurvy's sceptre from this ship.
We must have ample greens.

BLIGH:
Aye, Captain Cook.

[Exeunt BLIGH and JAMES KING]

COOK:
There flies a thrilling tale about these isles.
The rum-hole rumour claims to know that this
Is where that dreadnought Beaumont was marooned,
Upon one lost rock in the azure sea.

CLERKE:
And who might he be?

COOK:
What, have you not heard?
Perhaps you are too young to know of him,
But Beaumont is the most nefarious
And bloody pirate of this century
That England's proud – or shamed – to have produced.

CLERKE:
His name has never reached mine ears before.

COOK:
He is no longer sailing, thankfully,
But in retirement lives, or so they say,
No one has seen him twenty years at least.
Time-fattened hearsay adds that he has wed
A native woman, in their island style,
And has become a chief, no less.

CLERKE:
Did you say his name was Beaumont, Captain?
The same as Yorkshire's crested family?

COOK:
Precisely. The blackest sheep they've bred in years,
Who proved to be a most ferocious wolf
Beneath the courtly hide of false nobility.

CLERKE:
What else is known of him?

COOK:
A novel's worth!
If ever someone sailed too close to th' wind…
His grand, patrician father, much disquieted
By his scion's endless whirl of passioned
But ephemeral romances –
Ranging up from maid and down from duchess –
And all, of course, with scandal keenly spiced,
Decided, when his son turned twenty-one,
To send him t' America, to relatives.
En route, his ship by pirates was waylaid:
By all accounts a violent affair.
Young Beaumont, though, lost nor his verve nor thrust
But killed the pirate captain in a duel,

Becoming thus their sequent leader.

CLERKE:
How,
Without him having been at sea before?

COOK:
That was precisely Beaumont's greatest gift!
Though neither tall nor strong, he always rose
Above the sea of people, even when
It was a restless sea of pirate brutes.
He'd lead whatever crowd Fate threw him in,
The clay that shapes the best of generals.
Such absolute belief his will would triumph,
That those 'round him could not imagine else,
And so it was. A voice of thunder, eyes
Which seared you when you glimpsed what burns
[within,
In bygone times, they'd call them prophet's eyes.
Perhaps it was the slight exterior
Which many caught off guard, for who would think
The will within was greater than the man?
A giant in a body tailored small.

CLERKE:
When did you meet him, Cook?

COOK:
I never did.
Our orbits never crossed, and I am glad.
An ancient sea-dog told me this, and he
Could swear upon the arm that Beaumont cropt
That every word he said was true as day.
And almost nothing blunted Beaumont's wits:
He learnt with speed the alleys of the sea,
To read the frescoed stars as though a map,
And all the crafts of navigation's art –
The instruments with which our ships can reign

121

And tame the furied freedom of the main.
What many take a lifetime's bitter tries
He verily devoured in few short weeks.
Then started nine most bloody years: the sea
Ran crimson everywhere that Beaumont went,
A ceremonial red carpet lain for him,
The pirate prince, demon of the deep!
A Noah's Ark of nations was his crew:
Some Africans, Italians, and else –
The sea unites all those who ride its waves –
There are no barriers, no boundaries,
No muddy strip to love as motherland,
No crown to which to swear allegiance.
They held up every major passageway:
West o' Malaya, East o' the Caribbees.
They say he robbed and killed with cold efficiency
The crew of twenty ships of every flag.
Then suddenly, at thirty, he retired.

     CLERKE:
Then he is roughly equal to your age.
Why, he might still be very much alive!
But why retire?

     COOK:
               Perhaps he had enough.
The blood-washed age of piracy has dried –
They're now a fortunately fading kind.
He doubtless felt the changing tide of time.
A fresher era's beam has lit our age.
These pirates shark-like flee from nets of laws,
To die in caverns dark below the waves,
Or stray to madness fearing for their hoard.
And th' evil great will garner least lament
For many wish that ropes extend their necks,
In London, Paris, gallows garnish.
When Beaumont left, his crew went with the wind.
Without command, the regiment is blind.

His dreaded mate is certainly alive.
He's living somewhere in the Antilles,
Now honest, but obscure – he fishes pearls.

        CLERKE:
Then why did Beaumont come so far away?

        COOK:
For he has more to fear. He's wanted more:
The briny seas preserved the butcher's crimes.
Some islands here remain uncharted yet.
What better place t' elude the reach of justice,
And quondam comrades come to scratch at scars?
Aye, those who blow the sails of memories
Which must seem painful, either through the guilt
Besmirching them with scarlet murder's hue,
Or vapoured glories that they set afloat anew
With proud-flown banners of success and youth.

        CLERKE:
What has become o' his treasure?

        COOK [laughing]:
                                What, indeed?
It stays one of the sea's best-guarded riddles,
A fabled goldfish never caught but ever sought.

        CLERKE:
Perhaps he has it with him still.

        COOK:
                                Lord knows.
This talk of him makes me believe he lives.
Somehow it seems unnatural to think
That anybody ever dies out here,
Yes, here, where thrusting plants and burning sun
Affirm all life with such exuberance.
But even if the treasure's lost in time,

A thousand pound reward still crowns his head.

CLERKE:
A thousand pounds! He's worth our while.

COOK:

He's not!

CLERKE:
But if you were to meet? What would you do?

COOK:
What can one do but gaze at th' rare beast?
Then leave him be: he's no concern of ours.
I never waver from a sacred path
That is enlightenment, discovery.
Each day the drapery's drawn back some more
To flaunt our planet's virgin mysteries:
The wonders of a masterpiece divine.
Three continents I've sailed, the fourth I've sought –
A Southern land that logic said exists –
And everywhere a perfect order found.
I ponder how this Beaumont in such order fits...
That sums the interest that I have in him.
To aim to capture him is not our end.

CLERKE:
Think you that any nightmares him beset?
Do shades of torment rob him of his rest?

COOK:
I'm certain that they do. Each night, no doubt,
His mind goes on a voyage without charts...

[Exeunt]

Scene 2

[A small hut towards the back of the stage. BEAUMONT is
sleeping inside in a hammock. Dawn is waking.]

{An eerie shadow-play commences – BEAUMONT's dream.
Subdued lighting. Figures clad entirely in black enter from both
sides of stage and wage a violent battle. Eventually the figures
representing the pirates win, and the other figures are chased
offstage. All but two of the figures exeunt – one represents
BEAUMONT, a smaller figure is the Cabin Boy. A chest and a
spade are dragged out of the shadows. The Cabin Boy mimes
digging. The two figures lower the chest down through the
stage trapdoor. Then, the BEAUMONT-figure pulls out his
cutlass. The youth looks at him. He mouths a word.
BEAUMONT hesitates. Then, he kills the youth, who also falls
through the trapdoor. The shadow-figure exits running.}

[The real BEAUMONT sits up with a terrible scream]

BEAUMONT:
'Tis always same, that dream, invariant!
The dark-born demons which at night emerge
And march and march like soldiers through my mind.
A clockwork torture, regimented guilt,
Quotidian, monotonous precision!
[Gets up]
Those countless, bloody battles, lightning brief,
But endless seeming, for it was in them
I lived my most intense. The thirst and lust
For th' ever-granted satisfaction of a win,
A feeling of invincibility
That fed off each success and fed the next.
The intervals of peace like stagnant waters sat
As life and time to nothing stilled,
And into torpid apathy dissolved.
Aimless, empty days, a soul's hiatus
As absent action wilted senses brisk,

A mighty empire's interregnum years.
But that was empire built on blood and greed,
Aye, blood and greed: perverse yet thrilling chase!
Despite the waters of this Paradise,
It took some time to gain ablution's grace
And scrub away the clinging slime of greed.
I washed out th' blood, but avarice still held me fast.
I left the ship but took the treasure chest.
The gems, those Satan drops, I had to have.
The em'rald green for greed, the ruby red for blood.
I could not summon up my will
To scupper th' past, the jewels cast in brine,
A royal ransom plucked from Europe's prime,
Which they, in turn, from starving commons pried.
I could not square the axe above that final thread.
Then came that night, the night I earned my curse.
I skipped the ship with but the cabin boy,
A lad of fourteen years or so,
We went together to sepulchre it,
And then... and then... I killed him. Took his life.
By logic lost he had to die for it,
To leave me as the only one who knew
Where hidden lie those blasted diamonds.
But when I slew him, O! Those eyes, those eyes!
A victim's eyes that meet the murderer's
And in that heightened moment truest burn
As they bequeath their final suffering
To th' other man. They were like Isaac's eyes,
Nay, Isaac never looked at Abraham
From off the stone with gaze so set to damn,
The blinding glare of truth accusing.
Those orbs have charred regret into my skin.
And when the blade had torn his life, he spoke:
The innocent who sentenced me to death.
A solitary word escaped his lips,
The softest breath emerging from a mouth,
For me though, 'twas a hurricane's mad howl,
A rumbling, imprecatory utterance.

Three letters, said as one but meant as millions.
A treasure of our clumsy lexic store:
Laconic but lamenting too,
Inquiring but reflective too,
For all he said was... why? No more than... why?
That 'why' has been resounding endlessly
Inside my head, returning, haunting me
And echoing within my hollow soul!
That 'why,' so deep, for I so shallow was!
Oh God! That 'why,' those eyes, the dream, my curse!
It rendered clear a cry that I had stifled,
Which I had tried so fervidly t' avoid,
A voice that has been screaming ever since.
If only I had heard it earlier...
The blast of battle blotted everything,
'Tis plain to see now how I needed it.
That voice denies in raging tones the peace
That should be recompense for flitted years.
Instead, I am a greying, broken man,
Dissolved by guilt, long sold to Hell.
But soft, for slumb'ring nature stirs in sleep!
The humblest drop of dew becomes a pearl
As sunrays' vanguard volley glances it.
That burning giant yawns as dawn ascends.
Soon all will don majestic Gloria:
The time my muse does bathe in painted waves.
Where is my trusted telescope? My friend,
My eye, yes, you and I have secrets shared...
[Picks up telescope, then lies down on the ground behind some
bushes. Looks intently through the instrument.]
Vision of celestial perfection!
She's beauty written, drawn and sung,
A paragon o' creation, sculpture carved in flesh!
A child of Venus and of Neptune's she:
The sea and love commingling in her blood.
But no, and no again! She's more than that!
The marble poems of antiquity
Are merely bug-rid hags to her compared!

127

When races mix, two strange extremes result:
The offspring both the parents will eclipse
In either ugliness or comeliness.
Yet she has paid for her unequal share
With muteness. No sweet voice with which to tempt,
But flesh that over-amply compensates.
Oh, how she looks just like her mother did!
Those breasts, those Junoesquely sculpted legs...
Now soon she will be taken 'way from me.
I've given Lani fatherly consent
That she may wed Manoa, th' warrior.
There's love abundant in that union,
And yet... and yet I still mistrust the boy.
He yearns to take my seat before it's cold,
Ambition's green vines o'er his scruples creep.

[Enter MANOA. He sees the figure lying face down. He turns
BEAUMONT over and holds a lance to his throat, but seeing
who it is, recoils in surprise.]

MANOA:
Kaimi!

BEAUMONT:
Bloody fool!
[Gets up]
How dare you hold a lance at me, your chief?

MANOA:
What are you doing here in this unwoken light?

BEAUMONT:
I'm free to do whatever pleases me!
[MANOA looks into the distance and sees LANI.]

MANOA:
The seeing-pipe.
[Takes it roughly and looks through it]

You're watching her again.

BEAUMONT:
She is my daughter and not yet your bride!

MANOA:
Beware, you do what is kapu.[6] We've shared
Our life with you, so must you share our laws.

[Exit MANOA]

BEAUMONT:
Presumptuous young wretch! He will menace me?
'Tis impudence that has outgrown the imp.

[Exit BEAUMONT]

Scene 3

[BEAUMONT's hut. Enter a Boy running.]

Boy:
Kaimi! Kaimi!

[Enter BEAUMONT]

BEAUMONT:
I am here. What is this noise?

Boy:
Three far-born men have come!

BEAUMONT:
                                          What men?

---

[6] The Hawaiian version of the Polynesian word 'taboo'.

129

Boy:
They are coming this way.

BEAUMONT:
Are they? Who can they be? Go, show the way.

[Exit Boy, running. Noises off.]

My apprehension has been wrestled down
By curiosity run wild: the only thing
That strengthens when unfed. They come!

[Enter JAVEED with two PIRATES, followed by many
Islanders]

Javeed! 'Tis you!

JAVEED:
                    Me... Captain Beaumont. Me.

BEAUMONT:
How long...?

JAVEED:
                    Oh, twenty years 'tis been.
Yes, twenty since we stopped for water here,
This very island. Then, when darkness dropped,
You bid us sail. 'Twas only on the seventh day
We courage raised to break your cabin's door,
But all there glared was a message writ in blood,
As was your style. I well remember it:
It said, "Sail on without me." That we did.
The current you had set us in was strong,
Too strong to face about and search you out.

BEAUMONT:
It wasn't just the ocean's current halting you.
The currents o' fear were equal strong.

130

JAVEED:
But I have come. No current kept me back.

BEAUMONT:
It took you twenty years to find your way?

JAVEED:
Those twenty years have taxed you more than me.
You're not the dreadnought Beaumont any more.
Who would fear you now?

BEAUMONT:
                                The distance you have come
Exceeds by far the smallness of your talk.
Is there reason for this visitation?

JAVEED:
I want to know where our treasure is.

BEAUMONT:
Our treasure? *Ours?* Mine alone, Javeed.
You got your share: not large, but fair. Where's that?
What have you done with it?

JAVEED:
                                I fished for pearls.
For years I ploughed the languid Antilles
In tireless quest of th' ocean's richest fruit,
The tiny artisans whose workshop is their shell.
But those pearls soon ended, and my fortune melted.
I sank in debt. The sharks of credit swarmed.
The blasted tub in which I limped this far,
Just forty creaking feet, none of them mine!
I need that money just to stay afloat.

BEAUMONT:
What would you do with it?

JAVEED:

                Why do I need it?

BEAUMONT:
No! Never use that word in front of me!
D' you hear me? Never! It's a word... a word...
That is forbidden here.

JAVEED:

                Forbidden? Why?

BEAUMONT:
Don't say it, damn you! Don't! I loathe that word.

JAVEED:
[Aside] The austral sun has patted Beaumont's head.

BEAUMONT:
But then, I need not ask. Your answer's plain:
You want the wealth to buy yourself a ship,
Return to th' easy lure of piracy,
The lazy, golden harvest got from crime.

JAVEED:
I tried to live by laws: they were not made for me,
Nor I for them. One had to give.

BEAUMONT:
An honest life eludes those rotten through.

JAVEED:
I'm not to blame! The world is more at fault.

BEAUMONT:
Don't paint the saint, you wretch. Those hues are false
From one whose brush was ever dipped in blood.

JAVEED:
And who here paints the saint?

BEAUMONT:
I'm not as you knew me.

JAVEED:
I laugh at that! No, your kind never changes.
Your past is not a skin that can be shed,
And let alone the past that's grown on you.
'Tis yours forever, like your face or mind,
In scars and fears most undeniable.
I've brought you gift of opportunity
To purge that past by giving me its spoils.
That is what keeps the past still close to you,
That box you do not need, with gold and sin
So overfilled. Get rid of it, for then
You will be freed yourself, 'twill let you flee
Along the winding halls of memory.

BEAUMONT:
But more will die! I'll be the debtor of those lives!
How can two decades' torment be condensed
Into some feeble suspirations o' words?

JAVEED:
Give it to me!

BEAUMONT:
No!

JAVEED:
Where have you hidden it?

BEAUMONT:
Get out! Get off mine island! Go, you scut!

[He takes a lance and holds it to JAVEED's throat. The two Pirates draw.]

                    JAVEED:
So this is where we stand.

                    BEAUMONT:
                                        You mongrel cur.

                    JAVEED:
Now hear me, Beaumont. Hear me well.
An English ship is sailing close to here.
You're wanted still in England, as you know,
And I can always go enlighten them
Exactly who you are and where you hide.

                    BEAUMONT:
I don't believe a breath of it. You'll never go,
For any true marine would take you first.

                    JAVEED:
No, Captain, you're a bigger catch than I:
A haul that wins in London knighthoods, fame.
To let me slip the net is lesser fault
For they will have you as the lofty prize.
You're forced to barter in exalted stock:
Your life or gemstone ransom. I give you
Until tomorrow. Choose or chosen be.

[Exit JAVEED with two PIRATES]

                    BEAUMONT:
Varlet! I curse the wind that filled his sails,
And dredged his worthless form before mine eyes!
The hateful wretch! The thing that jars me most
Is that he read me with such ease. He palped
My rawest guilt. Can what he says be true?
For rumours dart about some visitors.

'Twas said they landed on the island's furthest end…
Or does he merely blow from whence the gust
I coldest feel? How can he be so free of guilt
While I am ripped between its reef-like fangs?
Or does this woe afflict the chosen few?

[Exeunt omnes]

Act II

Scene 1

[Enter JAVEED with two PIRATES]

> JAVEED:
> I've never seen him thus before,
> A pale impostor of the champion I knew.
> The suns that were his eyes in twilit gloom
> And every wrinkle writ with grief and fear.
> Mine envy almost cheers to pity now,
> For time has softly whittled him away,
> Like pyramid erased by the simoom.
> I chose my moment well, for now to him
> I am the Second Coming's threat fulfilled.
> What heathen half-belief he must have had
> Of leaving time behind with places, men,
> I have dissolved with every breath I've taken since.
> Yet still I wonder how it is
> That souls can rot before the body stills.
> Methinks it is this ceaseless sunshine's bright
> Against the chasmal blackness deep inside
> Which made him sterner judge above his wrongs.
> But now it serves me excellently well,
> For it is easier to lay a hand
> Upon his throat while he is on the ground.
> I'll catch him at the game I've seen him play,

Press the secret's juice from him, by thunder!
He measured others' greatness by his own
And even now 'tis me who waits for him,
When he should fear of me instead. Perchance
A pondered night has given him the time
To forge a fresher strategy, recover strength?
Or if he feels he's under siege,
He might set better guard beside his words.
Did I too proudly swagger on the warpath?
Did my threat and stifled cry of triumph
Lift him up or push him further down?
I'll know it soon, for here he comes. But soft,
Is that an angel gliding at his side?
Who is that being of another world?

[Enter BEAUMONT and LANI]

        BEAUMONT:
This is my daughter, Lani.

[She bows to JAVEED, who repeats the action.]

        JAVEED:
[Aside]   Rare to mine eyes.

        BEAUMONT:
So like her mother, she who gave her all
To let this child instead see light and life.
She's mute, alas. Go child, I'll follow soon.

[Exit LANI]

        JAVEED:
The spell is broken as she leaves.

        BEAUMONT:
                 Indeed,
A parting kiss enfolded in my sigh.

But I'll tell you where to find that coffin o' coins.

JAVEED:
[Aside] A cunning smile is playing by his eyes.
But what the Devil can it mean?   A gloat
Upon the crookedness of his chicane?

BEAUMONT:
I'll say this only once, so listen close:
  "When one, it has but one.
  When two, each too has two
  But when there's three or more,
  Each still has three and never four."

JAVEED:
Blasted scoundrel! Damn you, Beaumont, damn you!

BEAUMONT:
I hand you wealth and get no thanks?

JAVEED:
You've told me nothing!

BEAUMONT:
                    Flog that nagging mind!
That rhyme will tell you where to search and find.

JAVEED:
I did not come to hear your bloody puzzles,
Now tell me plain and clear the place to dig!
Don't murk the meaning with such double words,
Or else I'll riddle you, with bullet-holes!

BEAUMONT:
You think there is no fight to be endured?
No walls to climb, no tears through which to wade
And stumbling walk the narrow alleys o' time
To get to what can change a thousand lives?

For if your wit's too weak to work it out,
Then you're a worm unworthy of such wealth:
A slug that creeping slimes the coins of gold
Which it desires, but cannot e'er deserve.
Who are you to think that I will hand you
Such vast, unbounded wealth? To give you leave
To command at will a force that can create
Or else destroy with shuddering great stroke?
The world's awash with avarice
And riches turn the rats to gods. I won't step back
To see their number further raised. Clear off,
Or I will give the islanders the sport
Of hunting you to most unpleasant death!
'Tis now the feast of Ku, the god of war,
And swine like you are often offered up to him.

[Exit BEAUMONT]

        JAVEED:
My hands could crush a cannonball with rage!
My fury's storm could sink a fleet of ships!
I will explode if I don't let it out!
[To PIRATES] Oh, let my fingers firmly close on steel
        This island I will turn to flesh and pulp!
        A blade, a blade to cool my wrath in blood!

[JAVEED tries to rush out with a knife, but the two PIRATES restrain him.]

        1ˢᵗ PIRATE:
Stay, Captain. Killing him won't get us far.

        JAVEED:
You'll have me raze my knees in begging him?
Or in my cabin fume his riddle's twists?
I'll put an anchor through the head that thought that up!
Now let me go, accurséd dogs!
I'll blast that Beaumont to his rightful hell

Of a hundred hungry octopi!

[SFX: Drumming starts in the distance.]

2nd PIRATE:
O hear the islands thunder with their drums!

JAVEED:
A pagan feast. Perchance 'twill do us well
To search his hut meanwhile in twilight's cloak.
I'm cert the chest itself is not kept here,
But note or map must still be showing. Find it!
[They enter the hut and start searching. JAVEED finds the
telescope.]
The same he used in roaring days of blood.
I see him standing high upon the bridge.
Below the eye that's looking through the glass
His mouth is curling in a cutlass smile,
The quarry drawing close and soon the claws
Will sink in wooden flesh to rip the hapless ship.
'Tis hardly odd that this was all he took
Besides the treasure when he fled that night.
Its glassy memory could witness bear
To countless scenes of mad depravity.
And then, of course, he knew the swiftest way
To blind a whole ship's crew: just take their eye.
[Looks through the telescope.]
I see now why he built his hut up here.
There's hardly corner on this isle
Obscured from this mechanic oculus.
Aye, there's the beach a-boil with revelry.
We'll learn his standing with his people now.
He sits upon a throne, unmoving, cold,
As if an island in their sea of glee.
Is he distraught or pensive? Either way,
'Tis not a man who's celebrating victory.
That is a prizéd card I hold,
But when to play it is a science too.

[Enter MANOA and LANI. They start to kiss, but suddenly LANI notices JAVEED. She gives a soundless scream and runs out. MANOA approaches them.]

JAVEED:
[To PIRATES] You stay concealed. If he accosts me,
[show.
'Tis good that I have traded me some words
With th' islanders of where we hid our ship. –

MANOA:
Why are you here? Kaimi said you went.
He also said that if you here returned,
We must not let you land again.

JAVEED:
He did?
[Aside] He has not ordered them to kill us. Why? –
And do you always do what he commands?

MANOA:
He is the chief. I must do his commands.

JAVEED:
What kind of chief is he?

MANOA:
A great one!
He's often saved us from the other tribes.
He wins our wars with nectared words, or else
With trickery that's sharper than a spear.
He's cowered all the villages that warred with us.

JAVEED:
But are you not ashamed before those tribes
To have a chief who is not one of you?

140

MANOA:
Not one of us?

JAVEED:
       'Tis odd a noble race like yours
Cannot among its numbers find
A chief as great as him. How can that be?

MANOA:
He's proved himself well worthy of our blood.
He came before my birth, and I'm no boy.
At first, some worshipped him as a great god
But then he wed the old chief's only daughter,
And time consumed the novelty he had.

JAVEED:
Were you to wed his daughter, you'd be next
As leader of your people?

MANOA:
             That I would.
And I will be. Soon.

JAVEED:
          Be not so certain,
For chance has many storms to sink our firmest plans.
I knew him well before he came to you,
He vowed the same to me, to make me heir.
His promise flits inconstant as a butterfly.

MANOA:
He would not bar our marriage.

JAVEED:
         No? Why not?

MANOA:
He loves his daughter like the waves the shore.

141

He would not grieve her by dividing us.

JAVEED:
On the contrary, there are some parents
Whose over-ardent love's a circle o' fire
From whence their children can't escape.
Or maybe he would rather use his child
To tame the thoughts of hawkish enemies
By giving her in marriage to some prince.

MANOA:
I've met that worry too.

JAVEED:
You see? With Beau... Kaimi naught is sure.
You're of an age already fit to rule.

MANOA:
I am.

JAVEED:
Maybe you'd rule as well as him.

MANOA:
Maybe I would.

JAVEED:
What stops you then?
You ought to press him gently to retire,
To spend his days in rest and cede his reign to you.

MANOA:
No. In our land, 'tis death that crowns the next.

JAVEED:
But not in his. The greyness of the hair
Will often deeper seep into the mind.
Old men become indifferent to all.

142

They spend their time in weighing up their past
Those memories stowed away in old sea chests,
Now opened in a cloud of dust and each within
With rheumy talons fingered, put aside,
Another taken. Kaimi may not want
To keep on leading any more.

MANOA:
He will not give it up. I know he won't.

JAVEED:
This is no question o' will, but rather force.
He can be shaped to see another way,
In that I may be able to speed your cause.
But neither have I sailed 'round half the world
Just out of saintly charity.
I want your help in kind, a fair exchange.
When first he landed here, he brought along
A large and heavy chest. 'Tis that I want.
Seek it in the toothless mouths o' your elders,
Poke their jumbled trove of recollections.
Where is it now? And did he ever hide
Some rolls like yellow leaves, with markings on them,
Made soon after he concealed the chest?

MANOA:
If I agree – and which I haven't yet –
Tell me then, how would you my cause advance?

JAVEED:
I'll pile on him such weights that make the greatest
                                        [crumble.
I'll scent 'round him the odour of his sins,
I'll make the burning sun a judge's glare.
He'll sicken of his power and hand you it.

MANOA:
But what if he –

JAVEED:
Come now, say you agree.

MANOA:
I do.

JAVEED:
'Tis well. A handshake bind our words.
In my land, this is how men seal their pacts.
Here, grip my palm and hold it hard, just so.
[They shake hands.]
Now we both know the other's strength of will.

MANOA:
We'll meet again in three suns' time.

JAVEED:
Adieu.

[Exit MANOA]

This boy will find our treasure's trail.

[Exeunt JAVEED and two PIRATES]

Scene 2

[Enter BEAUMONT and the KAHUNA]

KAHUNA:
A crowd of years has filed by us
Since last a sacrifice we held. 'Tis time.

BEAUMONT:
Nay, hold. The men who came have brought ill winds.

KAHUNA:
That only heaps more reason on my side.
A feast like this will scatter gathered clouds.
Besides, you claimed those men would bow to you.

BEAUMONT:
They do. Those scabbards worn with flaunt and pride
Are hanging limp and empty at their side.
For what cause must you kill when all is calm?
Let wars pluck lives. Don't stab our fragile peace
With voices rancouring in agony.
Please...

KAHUNA:
I confer with gods. I know their wish.

BEAUMONT:
What slayful gods are these that joy in blood?
The one I know abhors such horrid acts.

KAHUNA:
Then your god merely *is*, while our gods *rule*.
Their power stops me questing for their reason.

BEAUMONT:
Pray, hold it off and wait a later date.

KAHUNA:
You have already won delay. Beware!
For danger stifling hangs within the air,
And great, mysterious events do stir
Which whisper bodings of convulsive times.

BEAUMONT:
I have no faith in those. It must not happen now!
I will not have you choose a man to kill.

KAHUNA:
It is not I who choose. They chosen are.

BEAUMONT:
Oh, can't you see the horror of it all?
What priest of grief are you to fray those cords
That firmly anchor souls to our sweet earth?
Will you cut free that rainbow-scope of sense
And let it float away t' oblivion?
And will you still those hands that shape the world
Or curdle the mighty mind that thinks and feels,
That masterfully reins the sails of reason?
A bloody rite that clips the stalk of life,
A feast of flesh for vengesome deities held,
It is not right and I forbid its pass!

KAHUNA:
But that will cause still more unrest.
You may be Chief, but I have powers too,
And mine are of a deeper world than yours.
I know, for one, your dream of yesternight
Was filled with ghosts of fresher smoke, not th' one
Recurring with the regularity of a tide
That's been your curse and custom long to see,
For nights and nights that spiral into years.

BEAUMONT:
By what unholy science know you that?
How could you see those raving shadows dance?

KAHUNA:
Our dreams are warnings from the gods,
And their unearthly kingdom is my realm.
I saw their form, but not their nature.
I did not see behind their ki'i[7] masks

---

[7] Commonly but mistakenly called 'tiki' – traditional Hawaiian wood carvings
of religious significance.

But knew they were the spirits of another plain.

BEAUMONT:
This is mirific knowledge for 'tis true:
My dream indeed did wear a new disguise.
The first I ever sailed was as a child.
'Twas when an uncle took me far to see
A fair but distant land called Italy.
We stopped in Venice, town of swan-like grace
That glides upon a glimmering lagoon.
Some steps beyond our dock, there was a house
Its windows always open thrown,
As if t' embrace the world that floated by outside.
[Music: Vivaldi's Violin Sonata Opus 2, Number 12, first movement]
And there, within, an old musician played
His face with care and age all faded, frayed
His hair once red, was waning into white
But still his hands possessed the steady strength
Which is a master's paltry recompense
For all the rest that age has robbed him of.
How wept that violin! What cries and sighs!
I heard it oft yet never took it in.
Much later, past a bitter harvest o' years,
As I was sitting in my cabin, it returned,
That trancing, rhythmic melody
In each long note a hundred sighs entwined
Accusing, pleading, aye, accusing me!
That violin, it cried instead of me.
Its colour th' oldest wine or driest blood,
Its player's mane a sadly dying fire.
With every note, majestically drawn
He deeper dug into my wretched soul.
That violin of Venice was to me
As doom-like as the trumpets o' Jericho:
I had to leave, to flee that crumbling world.
That's how I landed here. In paradise!
But now it came again, the requiem

Sung for the long procession of the dead
Who filed past me with mocking, gaping wounds
Within the torment of my dream. Where now?
The only way to leave this world as well
Is exit through the flame-jawed gate of Hell.
What other way to strangle th' abhorrent incubus?

KAHUNA:
Appease the spirits with an offerance.

BEAUMONT:
A curse on your oblation!

KAHUNA:
                              Softly tread.
You cannot scale the forces that you bait.

BEAUMONT:
No, you must speak to our High Chief, not me.
The Ali'i Aimoku[8] stands highest.

KAHUNA:
I know how much he leans on your advice.

BEAUMONT:
As now I ponder this, there is a way
Across this nettled maze of many claims.
You foretell that death will shake our island?
That murder's choking shades will visit us,
Dark out the life-beams of the sun? That must not be.
Now here's what I propose: 'The first to kill
Another on this island shall be yours
To offer to the gods.' A just exchange.
This shall proclaiméd be to everyone.
Perchance they will be slower reaching for their spears
When such an edict leers on reckless acts.

---

[8] Beaumont is a local chief, and lower than the High Chief or King.

[Exit BEAUMONT]

KAHUNA:
My purpose tripped to fall again. And yet
I do admire your skill in causing that...

[Exit the KAHUNA]

Scene 3

[Enter MANOA and Two OLD WOMEN. They sit on the
ground in a circle]

1st WOMAN:
So what do you want to ask us, handsome?

MANOA:
Are you the oldest in the village?

2nd WOMAN:
They say Hiapo is older, but he's so old that he's become a child
again.

MANOA:
Do you remember the day when Chief Kaimi first arrived?

1st WOMAN:
How can I ever forget? I have never seen so large a canoe. A
forest of masts and kapa-sails it was.

2nd WOMAN:
They stayed some days and came ashore a few times. So much
clothes on them, as if they'd never tasted sunlight. And so many
colours, they were as bright as parrots.

1st WOMAN:

Those clothes were a waste of time. They could never find their way out of them quickly when they wanted to play or swim.

MANOA:

What about the Chief?

2nd WOMAN:

He wasn't like the others. We could all see he was their leader. He was so serious and quiet, like he still is.

1st WOMAN:

But we all knew that he liked Anuhea, Lani's mother. Her father, the chief before him, didn't want her with the pale men, so he kept his distance.

MANOA:

What happened when they sailed?

2nd WOMAN:

We woke up one day, and their ship was gone. Like a rain cloud, it vanished between sea and sky.

1st WOMAN:

A few days later we found the Chief in one of the caves, upon the far end of the island. He had come ashore in one of the smaller boats and stayed.

MANOA:

Was he alone?

1st WOMAN:

I think he was with a kaua[9] boy, but the boy disappeared.

2nd WOMAN:

Maybe he tried to swim after the ship and drowned.

---

[9] Slave. The Hawaiians mistook junior sailors for their captain's slaves.

MANOA:
What about the smaller boat?

1st WOMAN:
It disappeared as well.

2nd WOMAN:
Maybe the boy took it when he went.

MANOA:
Was there anything else? Like a square wooden pot with a cover for keeping things?

1st WOMAN:
Pot?

MANOA:
Something large and heavy?

1st WOMAN:
I can't remember anything like that.

2nd WOMAN:
I think there was.

MANOA:
Yes or no?

2nd WOMAN:
Yes.

1st WOMAN:
No.

MANOA:
Oh, I should have asked the wind.

1st WOMAN:
So young and so rude!

151

MANOA:

How did you greet Kaimi after his ship had gone?

2nd WOMAN:

We didn't go near him for a while. He was so agitated, like some angry god.

MANOA:

Did he ever make any markings on yellow leaves?

1st WOMAN:

Yes. I saw him doing that later, when he had become the chief. Such a strange skill.

2nd WOMAN:

So many amazing things Kaimi's people could do. But none of them seemed happy. Their minds must be too crowded with magic.

MANOA:

Those leaves, where did he put them?

1st WOMAN:

I think he hid them under one of the stones on the floor. Maybe under one of the ones in the corner. I saw him replacing it once.

MANOA:

In the corner?

2nd WOMAN:

Why do you want to hear these stories now? You've never been interested in them before.

MANOA:

It's those men who left yesterday. I wanted to know what the ones before them were like.

2nd WOMAN:

The leader of those who came now was here with Kaimi the first time he came so long ago.

MANOA:

[Aside] So that's where they know each other from.

1st WOMAN:

Now that we've answered all your questions, do we get a lomilomi massage?

MANOA:

What?

1st WOMAN:

Come on, give your aunt a nice massage with those strong hands of yours.

MANOA:

No!

1st WOMAN:

No? You make us talk for no reward? What kind of man are you?

[Exit MANOA]

2nd WOMAN:

You've scared him off. He likes the women he massages to be young and firm.

1st WOMAN:

Oh, if I were young and firm, he wouldn't escape so easily. Ha!

2nd WOMAN:

Lani should take better care of him.

[Exit the Two OLD WOMEN, enter MANOA from the opposite side]

MANOA:
I'd rather clean a pigsty with my tongue!
Beneath a corner stone, she said. I'll look.
[He goes into the hut and soon emerges with parchments]
This must be what he wants. That simple stone
Beneath which these were hid has raised me up a step
To better reach my rightful sphere.
It is the whetstone of my chiefly spear.

[Exit MANOA]

Scene 4

[Enter BEAUMONT]

[Lighting FX: The sun goes down during this monologue.]

BEAUMONT:
Pursued I am, by men as much as ghosts,
Without reprieve or pardon's blest retreat.
I wander on the beaches, haunted, chased
A fugitive o' the sun's imputing raze.
These many enemies, encentred on a point
And from a compass of directions and intents,
Whose cannon hits the target first? By whose
Shall I be cut to fall? There's four on one:
That rat, Javeed, who speaks and breathes greed;
That looming English ship he claims is near –
Or is that empty threat to fill mine ear?
I've heard about a landing elsewhere...
Would they come so far to hunt my shadow?
There must be game that's readier
On th' Eastern stretch of Africa, or in the Caribbees,
Unless the world has shivered off its ills

And that I doubt. There's next that thrusting boy,
Whose looks are like the stings of rays,
Each hungry minute makes him deadlier.
And now this mystic madman, charlatan
With zealot's eyes and sanguinary drives
Who says he knows the gods and reads my dreams.
With what ghosts is he in communion?
Or is this further, darker treachery?
I can believe no more the words of men.
The people worship here a pantheon of gods:
The war-god, love-god, sea-god, rain-god:
There are four-hundred forty-four of them,
An ever-frothing brew of heroes, lusts
And jealousies, so like the Argives had,
Cerulean mirror held t' our mortal lives,
For every empire has their own: 'tis how
We can complete th' unfinished in ourselves,
That deeply human need to know a truth,
Believe in something that eternal seems.
The cheapest trollop in the gutter still believes
Survival worth the humbling shame.
The richest merchant craves still greater wealth,
And supplicates before his jingling god.
So long have I been here, I've lost all faith,
If that I ever had. Yet how I need
A purpose, just to cork the screaming void,
The vaguest o' reasons, slimmest o' straws to hold
And pull my spirit to some safety, to
A rock within the racing stream of hours.
To leave oneself to life's cascade
Means drowning in its anonymity.
Against these qualms wise Solomon exhorts:
"We were born by chance, and after life is over,
We will become as if we never had been born.
Our breath is but a puff of smoke, our mind
The spark thrown off by th' beating of our heart.
And when that spark dies out, our body will
To ashes crumble, and our breath become

155

A part of empty air. In time,
None will remember any of our works,
Our very names will flit into forget.
Our lives will pass away like traces o' clouds,
And vanish like mist in the heat of the sun.
Our time on Earth is but a passing shadow..."[10]
The purpose of it all must surely be
To carve a slice out of eternity,
However tenuously tiny, one
Which nonetheless will be a sign, a mark
A blink in all this vacant blackness, like the stars
Upon the dark, dark drapery of time.
Does each one shine for some unending life?
Were they made by th' arrows of our giants?
Then where am I within this void? Still young,
I shot mine arrow at that nothingness.
Methought the strength of youth would speed it best.
I fired it far and up, but left no trace,
Except the trace of bodies it ran through.
Beyond recall, its path remains to scorn,
Its trajectory an indelibly bloody scar.
'Tis far too late to aim again, to set
A fresher shaft to string and point it at
The monsters that the first one did unleash.
Too late, I've shot my bolt, no arrow's left:
The quiver of each life holds only one.
So I am spent, now nothing but a shell
That's washed by rolling tide, the planet's pulse,
And lies upon the bottom of a puddle.
I see the sky, but I can no more reach for it.
What's left for me to struggle for? Now even here,
The purest Eden known to living men,
The land beside the sunset, even here
The serpent has arrived to coil and kill.
Modernity's skilled greatness only loans us
Still crueller ways to gorge our petty selves,

---

[10] Wisdom of Solomon 2:2-5 paraphrased

We animals of false nobility!
We human beasts, in our academies,
Still haven't learnt to add up all our flaws.
Better I see men as subtle shades of evil
And by the rare exception be
Most pleasantly surprised, than see them sweet
And everywhere with disenchantment meet.

[Enter LANI]

You step so lightly, nymph. But come, approach.
Your angel presence lights my guilty shade.
Perhaps you've rescued me from worse. You are
The only thing I've done without regret.

[Exeunt BEAUMONT and LANI]

Scene 5

[Enter JAVEED and Two PIRATES]

JAVEED:
Where is the lad? This is the time and place.
Has he been snared while searching for the map?
Perchance he's not the weapon of first choice.
If Beaumont does suspect our daring game,
He'll know the boy's ambition is the knife
With which he might be stabbed.

[Enter MANOA with the parchment]

You're here at last!
What took so long?

MANOA:
I have the thing you crave.

157

JAVEED:
Good! Give it to me! Ah! The parchment's old.
But what in thunder are these signs?

2nd PIRATE:

A code!

JAVEED:
Yes, I can see that it's a bloody code!
The cunning fox! Can you unravel it?

2nd PIRATE:
'Twas you what sailed with him. Did you not share
His secret ways?

JAVEED:
He handled those with thrift.
A private pirate. What else did you glean?

MANOA:
I spoke to two o' the oldest women here
Who were alive when Beaumont first arrived.
But you know how he landed, you were with him.

JAVEED:
I was.

MANOA:
Then why did you not return for him?

JAVEED:
Why? There are things that you won't understand.

MANOA:
Indeed? And there are things that I won't tell!

JAVEED:
If you know him, you must the answer know.

158

We feared him. He'd such power over men,
That none would dare his purpose cross.

      MANOA:

                                  And now?

      JAVEED:
He's altered, weakened by his age and guilt.
Now you and I can rise to challenge him,
If we exchange our trust, unite our strength.
So tell me what he did with th' heavy chest.

      MANOA:
They said he stayed at first within a cave
Down by the rocks, with a boy from th' ship.
One day the boy and... "chest" ...both disappeared.

      JAVEED:
Where is that cave? We'll search it quick!

      MANOA:
'Tis on the island's distant shore, and hard to find.

      JAVEED:
It might repay our while to look. What else?

      MANOA:
To cross the straight from there won't raise a sweat.

      JAVEED:
Yes, and he had the longboat from our ship.
It could be on the island next to this.
But it's a large one. Still they could not have
Advanced too far with such a weighty load.
Are there any caves?

      MANOA:
                  I do not know of any.

JAVEED:
Damn! Did he never speak of what he'd done?

MANOA:
Those women don't remember anything.

JAVEED:
He has not dropped a crumb for hungry ears.
Upon those parchments I will have to pore
And hope to smooth their wildness into sense.
By thunder, even if I stare at them
Until my eyes dissolve to salty pools
I fear no glint of meaning will I see.
There's no two clues to strike together and
To kindle hope from them. How ran his rhyme?
      "When one, it has but one.
      When two, each too has two
      But when there's three or more,
      Each still has three and never four."
What has but one thing when it is alone?
A beggar and his penny? But two each have two.
Two what? Arms, eyes? But when there's three or
                              [more...
It merely multiplies its mysteries!
What in blazing hell means that conundrum?
We'll have to find another way into his world.
What is the thing he dearest holds?

MANOA:
Lani.

JAVEED:
Precisely. His daughter.

MANOA:
                  And my bride.

JAVEED:
Then it is her we'll use to get to him.

MANOA:
Use Lani? She would never him betray!
The cords that them together bind
Are spun from thickest twines of love and care.

JAVEED:
Betrayal is not needed. No, instead
We'll use her as the bait to snare him with.

MANOA:
I do not like the pattern of this plan.
To force a child to cause her father's fall
Will crease her brow with ugly bitterness.
And what if harm should come to her?

JAVEED:
Nay, wait.
You don't yet know my plan by stroke and trick.
Two large ships are now circling 'round these isles,
As great as th' one on which Kaimi came.
They've come exploring from his land of birth
And soon they'll drop their anchors here as well.
If we infect him with the thought these ships hunt him,
He'll soon be conquered by his fright's disease,
Transfixed like prey by two voracious eyes.
And once they realise just who he is,
They'll surely wrench the secret from his mouth,
As if it were the finest ivory.
We'll then but need to ambush th' party sent to dig.
And as for you, a throne will waiting stand.

MANOA:
What if he holds?

JAVEED:

                We can then rescue him
And give much cause for him to feel obliged.
'Tis smooth and simple as a pearl!

MANOA:

                        Perhaps,
But where does Lani enter into this?

JAVEED:

That's where the finery is woven in.
We'll make him think the English mariners
Have captured Lani and she will be killed
Unless he ransoms her with his own life.
Instead she'll be concealed in some safe place,
Released when Beaumont's folded in our net.

MANOA:

Why do you not just tell him you took her,
And not involve the foreigners from his land?

JAVEED:

I must pretend to set them on his tracks,
For if I don't, he'll make them search for me.
What's more, I'd rather he knew not at first,
But felt it like a bullet when too late,
Perish with the thought of being bettered...
'Tis excellent design, for in this way –

MANOA:

She need never know the truth
About her father's end and how I played a part.

JAVEED:

Just so. My men will spring and capture her
When she's alone.

MANOA:
          And where will she be hid?

JAVEED:
My ship's secure.

MANOA:
          Will she be treated well?

JAVEED:
Just like the princess that she is!

MANOA:
                 Beware.
If one of you so much as dare her touch,
I'll dig his rotten heart for trophy out.

JAVEED:
Come now! We trust each other, do we not?
We'll guard her as a royal prisoner.

MANOA:
I'm most averse to using her like this.
The losing of her father t' orphancy
Exceeds already what she ought to bear.

JAVEED:
But then she will have you to compensate.
She's requisite for this design. Who else,
Who else can move him more?

MANOA:
               Let it be so.
May it flow as well in deeds as in your words.

JAVEED:
It will! The gambit move is seizing Lani.
It must be done as soon as they come near,

We'll list with vulpine ears for th' anchors' plash
But it's your work to lure her somehow here.
We'll do the rest. I'll leave a message in the sand
Writ for Beaumont, seemingly from th' English.
Make sure that it's not trampled ere 'tis read.
To fetch the English here with quicker speed,
Provoke them somehow – filch perchance a boat.

      MANOA:
I will.

      JAVEED:
Now onward to success!

      MANOA:
                  To it!

[Exeunt JAVEED and the Two PIRATES]

I stand about to dive in murky waves.
I've never done a thing like this before,
The weaving of such a wickerwork of lies.
But now, I'll force her to captivity
And be the priest who summons him to death…
How will I share my mind with such an act?
And what if Lani learns of it? That man,
Can he be trusted with mine honour's bond?

[Exit MANOA]

Scene 6

[Enter BEAUMONT, looking through a telescope]

      BEAUMONT:
The fountain o' light has surged to th' highest point
For dawn has reached its colourful eclipse,

The wonder of th' eternal fireworks' nearly spent,
Yet she's not here. She does not grace the waves
To race the chariot of Helios
In their amazing match of perfect bright.
Where is my mermaid? Where? I scan in vain.
This habit's not been broken for a day
Since many years. What's caused this disarray?
But hold! What's stirring there? Two ships!
Two ships! What flag? An English one. O woe!
They're here for me. They must have come by night.
The skies have dropped this dreaded day at last!
It was an omen that my angel did not walk.
What are the names o' these vessels grim as doom?
Discovery and *Resolution*. Meant for me.

[Enter the KAHUNA, the Two OLD WOMEN, NOHEA and other Islanders]

KAHUNA:
The two ships came by night. You've seen them, too?

BEAUMONT:
I have. Yes.

1st WOMAN:
Shall we welcome –

BEAUMONT:
No! let them not land!

2nd WOMAN:
Let them not land? But they've already spent
Some nineteen days on th' island's other end.
Their leader's Lono, god of potency.

BEAUMONT
[Aside] He bloody well is not. He's here for me.

165

NOHEA:
What does our chief command?

BEAUMONT:
                              Command? Oh God!
I'm in no state to even rule myself!
[Aside] I cannot stall their purpose anyway,
So let them come. I've had the luck of ten. –
But tell the King to treat them frigidly,
And keep your distance from them, all of you!
Don't voice a single word about myself,
Not even if they ask. They want my head…

KAHUNA:
What are these ships that strike you pale with fright?

BEAUMONT:
They are the solid form of hell-yawned dreams.
Have any come ashore?

2nd WOMAN:
                              Not yet.

BEAUMONT:
                              They will.
Where is my daughter? Who saw Lani last?

NOHEA:
I saw her by the well last night.

BEAUMONT:
                              She must be found!

KAHUNA:
What makes you think she's disappeared?

BEAUMONT:
                              I know 't.

166

1st WOMAN:
Perhaps she's with Manoa.

BEAUMONT:
Find him too.
He's lately acting fugitive.

KAHUNA:
Your limbs and voice are shaking both – what for?

BEAUMONT:
I want the island searched for both of them,
Across and through. Go raise a cry and gather men!

[Exeunt most]

KAHUNA:
I cannot understand the cause of this.

BEAUMONT:
You claimed to know my spirit: read me now.

KAHUNA:
'Tis clouded –

BEAUMONT:
Aye, with consternation's haze.
Where is my daughter, th' angel of the sands?
The only gem that lit my weary crown.
And where's the boy? Impulsive rogue!
Could he have pressed her into flight with him?
O may the sun chase 'way the shadows that her mask!

[Enter MANOA]

2nd WOMAN:
Here comes Manoa now.

KAHUNA:

> Where have you been?

BEAUMONT:
[Aside] Mayhap it has not happened after all. –
Where is she?

MANOA:

> Falsely taken prisoner.

BEAUMONT:
What do you say?

NOHEA:

> A prisoner?

KAHUNA:

> But how?

MANOA:
I saw her being captured by a pack.
They put her in a boat and rowed towards their ship.
I tried to give them chase, but they had rods
Of taméd fire.

BEAUMONT:

> To which ship did they row?

MANOA:
The closer one to us.

BEAUMONT:

> The *Resolution!*

KAHUNA:
They've never taken one of us by force before.

BEAUMONT:
How right was I to sense that this would pass,
But I would have rather been mistaken,
Than this oracular foreknowledge proven right.

[Enter a Man]

Man:
We're searching still, but there's no sign of Lani.

BEAUMONT:
So it is true! They've taken her.

MANOA:
They left some drawings in the sand.

BEAUMONT:
What's that?

MANOA:
Strange marks.

KAHUNA:
A message?

MANOA:
It spoke not to me.

BEAUMONT:
Where are those marks? Come, lead us there and quick!

[Exeunt omnes on one side of stage and re-enter on the other]

MANOA:
This is the place.

BEAUMONT:
The closest point towards their ship. What says 't?

"We have your daughter, Beaumont. She will die
Within 3 days unless you give yourself up."

MANOA:
Die? That word's the cry of war! She must be rescued!

BEAUMONT:
"We have your daughter, Beaumont." No reprieve…
So clearly writ for me, it even notes my name.
There's not the faintest glow of living hope
That this was done in error. It was not.

MANOA:
Let's charge their ship at night. We'll burn them all!

BEAUMONT:
Rash words!

MANOA:
    But we can take them!

BEAUMONT:
          No, we can't!

MANOA:
Are you afraid?

BEAUMONT:
    Less foolish than I'm brave!
Do you not think they are prepared for that,
For such contingency? They've cannonry
To blast you out of life with smoke and rumble!
Those gaping, dragon maws of firing rows,
Each barrel is a tunnel unto Hell!

MANOA:
Then you must surrender to them, as they ask.

BEAUMONT:
And who are you to circumscribe my acts?

MANOA:
Do you have choice? They'll kill her if you don't.
Or does your selfishness discount that thought?

BEAUMONT:
Begone, you wretch! How dare you? All of you!
Away! Go! Leave my sight! I need to think
Without your ceaseless buzz. [To the KAHUNA] And
                                              [you as well!
I need no magic, just the fortress of my wits.

[Exeunt omnes, save BEAUMONT]

"We have your daughter, Beaumont. She will die
Within 3 days unless you give yourself up."
'Tis terse and deadly like a viper's kiss,
Or verdict for an execution.
It marks the place whence she was seized. It gives
What they have done, and now what I must do.
The rules of bargain, nay, the terms of sale.
It gives the when and who and what of death,
A death which can averted be, or rather,
Delayed by much if I will acquiesce.
What is the nature of the men that crouch
Behind these leering letters, stark and bold,
Here scrawled into the sands of time itself,
Where each minutest grain, in all its tininess
Does play a part in making up a striking whole?
My life is dust to me, but hers is gold.
If only I had been instead out here
Upon this boiling beach when demons crept,
The trailing tragedy that's been my life
Would have at last received its final point,
An almost elegant conclusion.
But with this deed, they've struck at more than me,

171

They've barged through fragile lacework in my soul.
How did they know this torment would be worst?
The snaking whip upon the bleeding back?
The Heavens surely cheer for my demise!
This is Justicia's sword descending doom.
That fearful force has whispered from above
The place where knives would deepest glide in me.
But no, I'm rambling like a country road.
It had to be our proxime enemies,
They must have landed there and heard the tale,
Or e'en Javeed could have implored himself on board.
Whoever did it stung me sharp.
They have marooned me on a pricky reef
Where tiding waters jumble o'er my head.
I can now start the count of melting hours:
Time then to cast a tearful, farewell gaze
Across the broad expanse that's been my life,
The oceans crossed and waves survived,
Their shadow valleys and their crags of deadly drops.
But will my fall attain the hallowed cause?
And her release procure? Or will it be
A vain campaign, quixotic to the end?
When I am caged by bars of metal fangs,
There won't be anything to warrant it
From ones who are already low enough
To sink to such most base, extortive means
And put a lamb upon the chopping block
To make its parent weakly bleat
And give itself away. The wormish thieves!
They wear their honour like a flea-rid cloak.
"We have your daughter, Beaumont. She will die
Within 3 days unless you give yourself up."
Yet even th' worst of roads will fork somewhere.
There must a channel be to navigate these straits.
But where? And can I gamble with a life
More sacred than mine own? Where hide my wits?
I must revive again that Beaumont spirit!
There's just the merest trine of days t' unreel

A Gordian of knots that's tied in steel.

[Exit]

Act III

Scene 1

[King KALANIOPU sits upon a throne surrounded by subjects on each side: Chiefs, the Two OLD WOMEN, NOHEA, the KAHUNA and others]

KALANIOPU:
I give you now the most miraculous
Invention that I've ever seen. Behold:
A form that's almost insolently simple
But whose abilities and properties
Are just an incantation short of magic.
These things can pierce and bind and even wound,
They can be used for anything one wants.
They can't be broken, burnt or bent
They're shiny, sharp and hard. They came to us
Upon the floating island standing in the bay,
And Lono's people call this wonder "nail."

[Holds up a large nail. It is passed around and examined carefully by everyone]

Look upon it well. What is it made of?

Old Chief:
It might be from the jaws of some great fish.

Another Old Chief:
Perhaps 'tis root of some uncommon plant.

173

NOHEA:
I got it from the Man who Works with Trees.
He said that underground it grows.

KALANIOPU:
How strange.

1st WOMAN:
Yes, yes. I did once see some bigger ones.
They grew like headless mushrooms in a cave
While others hung above like lethal spears.
They weren't so beaming, but the shape was same.

NOHEA:
The Man who Works with Trees has many tools,
And most are made from this material.
He uses one to beat the nails in place,
Another one can pull them out again.
The most amazing thing I've seen him do
Was when he held a nail above a flame.
It changed its colour to a glowing red
And he could twist it while its light remained.

KALANIOPU:
I want you all to gain these if you can,
And try to glimpse the many ways and means
That Lono's host does work and master it.

KAHUNA:
I've matters to discuss, Your Majesty.

KALANIOPU:
Then speak.

KAHUNA:
It is for royal ears alone.

[Exeunt omnes, save the KAHUNA and King KALANIOPU]

174

You called the leader of those people Lono.
Do you therefore believe that he's a god?

KALANIOPU:
I haven't yet decided it. But you,
You doubt his godliness.

KAHUNA:
                    I do.
Does he behave at all like Lono would?
Our customs strike him silent with surprise,
When he should know them well. How can that be?
What's more, our language he can barely speak.

KALANIOPU:
He speaks the language of the gods. We don't.
His manner, that's most ceremonious.

KAHUNA:
Not one of his escort calls him Lono.
Instead, strange names like 'Captive,' 'Cuckoo,' 'Sore.'

KALANIOPU:
What of the legend from the dusty past?
The ancients have foretold that he'd return.
They said he'd come upon a floating isle:
Those grandest vessels well deserve that name.
They said he'd round our island thrice, then land.
He did just so. And even those three posts
Which stand upon his vessel are arranged
Exactly into Lono's sign as proof.

KAHUNA:
But why come back, return a second time?
When first he came, it was upon the very day
That Lono's festival begins to pulse.
A thousand people cheered and greeted him,

And no one faltered hailing him our god,
Fulfilling that most antique prophecy.
But now, his visit is at odds with th' moods of stars.
It is not right.

KALANIOPU:
He has to be a god!
He bears the greatness of another world.
He can command with sureness many men,
And summon up the wonders of such things
Whose natures comprehension fierce defy.
His powers are tremendous, frightening!
If, as you suppose, he is not Lono,
Then what pretender or impostor's he?
Who can he be if not a god?
No ordinary man is so distinct.

KAHUNA:
Though I can't counter that, my doubts persist.
Our Lono is the god o' fertility.
Yet of our daughters who his escort pleased,
Full twenty have been cut with illnesses
With which we've never been beset before,
And which confound our herbalists. Some died.
I'm led to think he's come to punish love,
And not to be its highest priest.

KALANIOPU:
Where is Kaimi when I need his counsel most?
He is our link to these new visitors.

KAHUNA:
He does his very best t' avoid this group,
Prefers instead to wander cliffs and caves.
There's something ominous between the two.

KALANIOPU:
A rumour's reached me of his daughter, Lani.

They said that Lono's host have captured her,
And want to barter her for him. Can this be true?
What does it mean? He must be found!

KAHUNA:
Do you have faith in *his* divinity?

KALANIOPU:
Perhaps… but only as a faded god.

[Exit King KALANIOPU]

KAHUNA:
If this false Lono stays, we priests will fade,
And something should be done to end his raid...

[Enter MANOA]

MANOA:
The third day, and Kaimi does not act.
He meanders restless high above the sea
With eyes unseeing, ears unhearing, lost to all.
What do you think is boiling in his mind?

KAHUNA:
Methinks what fumes within is brew so strong,
That it would poison lesser minds. He walks,
With paces strong, for when the soul's entrapped,
The body will more freedom seek
To countervail the loss of one with th' other's gain.

MANOA:
But will he go to be their prisoner?

KAHUNA:
Perhaps not even he knows that as yet.
How can I scan his thoughts when those are still
A swirling, unresolvéd mass?

MANOA:
Why speak you not to him, and urge him to depart?

KAHUNA:
You've seen his state. He cannot be approached.
Besides, why should I force him so to act?

MANOA:
You've often said, the gods are stirring. Who,
Who else can be the cause of that but him?

KAHUNA:
I doubt that is the case. There's something more,
A great destructive force, entwined in words,
Enwrapped in thoughts.

MANOA:
                          'Tis fear of Kaimi.
He has been chief too long. Consider it:
We've had our people's order for so long,
A thread of lives that in their length
Can wind their way to time-enmisted myth,
Order that's divine in its perfection.
But he, who comes from far, tore through our sails.
He is an outsider who has capsized
The balanced custom of a thousand years,
And we have let ourselves be thus misled.

KAHUNA:
Where is this new-sprung hatred bursting from?
You were not one for such disloyalty.
He's ruled with fairness, kept our foes in check.
There's few of us who could have better done 't.
Besides, who could be chief if he is gone?

MANOA:
I'm right for it.

KAHUNA:
        [Aside] Ah, now 'tis clear. – Why you?
We've countless dauntless warriors, and sages
Rewarded with the prize of wisdom gained
By virtue of their many years, why you?

MANOA:
Had he not come, my father could have been
The chief through marriage to Anuhea.
What's more, I've royal blood enough in me
T' ascend those sacred steps too long defiled.

KAHUNA:
There's royal blood in all of us, if one
Is desperate for it.

MANOA:
        I will his daughter wed.

KAHUNA:
If she is returned alive.

MANOA:
        She will be.

KAHUNA:
He thinks it might be otherwise. That's why
He cannot fold decision either way.

MANOA:
I have foreknowledge that it will be so.

KAHUNA:
Since when do you engage in prophecy?
And if you see him such a baleful force,
Is Lani not the same, she who is
His flesh and blood?

179

MANOA:
                    But only half of her.
The other half is true to us.
The good must range themselves behind my lead,
For that I your assistance do entreat,
Kahunas have the people's eager ear.
And you could also speak to him
To reconcile him gently to the thought.
Ours would be invincible alliance.

KAHUNA:
I do not get involved in mortal struggles.
My duty is to higher beings alone.

MANOA:
I will restore the ancient right. See how
He calls upon the gods of his old world
In direst times. I'll have respect for ours,
And you, the main minister of the faith.
Your calling, too, would greatly benefit.
You'll be rewarded richly when I rule.

KAHUNA:
I do not choose my actions by reward!

MANOA:
You also fear him.

KAHUNA:
                    Neither him, nor you.

MANOA:
Think on it. My lead's the one to follow.

[Exit MANOA]

KAHUNA:
Go play with brightest light. I'll watch from far,

And out of shadows deep I'll timely stride
When you've extinguished it, or been made blind.

[Exit the KAHUNA]

Scene 2

[SFX: Ship noises: straining rigging, creaking wood]

[The dark hold of Javeed's ship. LANI is tied up by some
barrels. Some empty rum bottles lie nearby. JAVEED descends
a ladder with a lantern.]

JAVEED:
Well, well, the rum has washed away your thirst.
No doubt you've never tasted it before.
It is like water to all sailing men,
So bitter that you can no longer taste
The biting bitterness that is your own.
And pirates are the bitterest of men,
That's why we need its acrid quench the most.
But best of all for current purpose,
Is that it swirls the present to a cloud,
And even when the fog has stolen off,
There's nothing in its place: an empty stage
No scenery, nor actors, just the vaguest sense
The memory of having seen a play,
But what it was forever will elude.
O how I hate and envy Beaumont's skill
In being best in anything he tried,
It seems that even fathering a child.
A masterwork you are, that's painted with
The finest blood of two disparate peoples.
But now, 'tis I who's proved the better, I,
The cleverer, the more resilient,
And so, I'll claim the victor's pleasure.
[The light is obscured. Darkness.]

Where are you now, Lord Beaumont? Where?
You're nothing but a shipwrecked argosy
That sailed and sank with equal spectacle.

[Exit JAVEED up the steps. He leaves the lantern behind.
LANI uses its flame to burn through the ropes. She rips off her
gag and exits]

[SFX: A splash.]

Scene 3

[SFX: Ship noises: straining rigging, creaking wood, cries of
gulls.]

[The *Resolution's* deck. Enter PHILLIPS from one direction
and VANCOUVER from the other a moment later.]

VANCOUVER:
Good morning, Phillips.

PHILLIPS:
Morning, sir. Sleep well?

VANCOUVER:
Yes, thank you. Where's the captain?

PHILLIPS:
Rather, how?

VANCOUVER:
What?

PHILLIPS:
It's not where, but rather how, he is.

VANCOUVER:
And how is he that's so peculiar?

PHILLIPS:
He's madder than a whale with eight harpoons in him.
I haven't seen him in a fouler mood
Since I have known him.

VANCOUVER:
                                        Not like him at all.

[Enter COOK]

COOK:
Good morning, Mr Vancouver.

VANCOUVER:
Good morning, captain.

COOK:
                                        Mr Vancouver,
Can a day go by without a theft?

VANCOUVER:
                                        Sir?

COOK:
I am upset beyond all measure. In th' night
A youth audaciously a cutter stole.
The sentry's fire deterred him not a jot.
Since landing on this isle a second time
We've suffered far too many of these acts.
That purloined cutter is the final straw!
I will not stand for this. I demand that it's returned.
Our froward situation's most abused.

VANCOUVER:
It is the metal that they crave.

183

COOK:

'Tis so.

On every other island that we've visited,
Those trinkets that we use as currency
Could endlessly enthral the local people.
Here, they disparage all such trumpery,
While metalwork is polished for them with
The tantalising glint of novelty.
Yet that won't balm my anger at being robbed!
I have a plan t' effect a quick return:
We'll seize canoes and seal the bay to all,
So naught that's waterborne may pass by us.
I want to make it daylight clear
That cutter is significant to us.

VANCOUVER:
[Points] I believe that's Captain Clerke approaching.

COOK:

Good.

Go tell him what has happened and what will.
This rare rage has made me less articulate.

[Exit VANCOUVER]

In spite of all, they're fascinating souls.
They share possessions with all countrymen
More readily than we with our own families.
They're th' only race of whom I can believe
They'd let a foreigner become a chief.
They lack a word for 'bastard.' Children are a gift,
And there's no circumstance to taint them sin.
Though we might see them, both in dress and love,
As nude in morals, surely we appear to them
As strangled by formality
And torn from nature's cradle. These islanders,
They've never known what's metal, but to us
'Tis sword and gun, and nails for the cross.

And what is gold and silver? Jealousy
That can be touched. What woeful images!
Are these the fruits of our advancement then?
These lands have shown, all nations so cut off,
Develop in their own divergent ways
With variant velocities in different directions.
For history doth travel without maps
And knows no paths that run in parallel
Nor speed that's shared. And yet there's order in 't…

[Enter CLERKE]

     CLERKE:
Good morning, or at least, a better one.

     COOK:
Good morning, Captain Clerke. Have you been told?

     CLERKE:
[Nods] The haste, though, of your plan a weakness
                               [seems.
Some more reflection ought to armour it.

[Enter JAMES KING]

     KING:
Good morning, sirs. I fear I drag bad news.

     COOK:
What, more? Bad news, it seems, accumulates
With th' quantity and constancy of flies
That crowd a carcass in the sun! But speak.

     KING:
A wild attack was sprung on us last night.
Our gunfire struck no dread into their hearts,
But fortunately they took very little.

COOK:
Decisive action's called for even more.

CLERKE:
I still believe the plan improvement begs.

COOK:
You're right. We'll take their king a prisoner
And keep him comfortably well immured
Here on the ship until they will relent.
Though it disturbs me much to have to reach
For such a risky, violent recourse,
It strikes me as the most expedient.

CLERKE:
Indeed, arrests have worked for us before.

COOK:
Aye. Mr King, return to shore. Once there
Dispense assurances to everyone you can
That no one will be harmed, no one at all.
I merely want to converse with their king.

KING:
Aye, aye, sir.

[Exit JAMES KING]

COOK:
            Captain Clerke, I think 'tis best
That you return to the *Discovery*.
Your illness surely demands you rest.

CLERKE:
When action's nearness tingles every nerve?
But yes, I'll try. For Heaven's sake, take care.

[Exit CLERKE]

COOK:
I'll take the tender and the launch. I'd say
A force of forty men is wisely sized:
Not large enough to stir suspicion's waves,
But neither small enough to sink in an assail.
[To PHILLIPS] Assemble all of the marines!
Quick, Phillips!

PHILLIPS:
Aye, aye, sir. All hands on deck!

[Enter BLIGH and Marines]

COOK:
Ah, Mr Bligh, I trust you've heard the plan?
I charge you with the closing of the bay.

BLIGH:
I won't let anybody out or in.

[PHILLIPS hands COOK a gun. COOK loads it.]

Are you not loading it with small-shot, sir?

COOK:
I pray to God I will not have to fire.
[To Marines] Our aim is not revenge, but property's
[return.
Don't for a moment let that slip your minds
In the next few hours.

BLIGH:
Very well, sir.

COOK:
Be niggards with bullets, and use them
Strictly for your own protection. Forward!

[Exeunt omnes]

Scene 4

[Enter BEAUMONT and a group of Islanders]

BEAUMONT: What hope, what miracle did I await?
What help from Fortune's hand or Godly frown?
There are no wonders for such sinners great
But th' wonder lightning never strikes them down.

I'll go. I have to go. My future's bare:
I'll cross at once the Rubicon and Styx.
Prepare a boat while I myself prepare
For torment worthy of the crucifix.

The carpenter who his own gibbet made
Is locked from life behind a shibboleth.
Now into this cathedral o' bones has strayed
A child I must deliver through my death.

To darkness I have ceded everything:
Come, silken noose, in wind me sweetly swing.

[Exeunt omnes]

Act IV

Scene 1

[The beach. COOK, PHILLIPS and other Marines alight from a small boat. Many Islanders approach.]

COOK:
[Shouting to Marines, offstage]
188

The rest stay waterborne, but keep us in your sight!
If you hear any trouble, land at once.

[The party walks circuitously towards King KALANIOPU's hut.
People prostrate themselves as "Lono" passes. The King's two
sons run to meet them.]

Boys:
Lono! Lono! Come with us.

[Each takes one of COOK's hands and leads him to the hut.
They scamper into it.]

COOK:
Phillips, go in there and bring him out.

PHILLIPS:
Captain, that would tramp upon their custom.

COOK:
Phillips, we are not here to be polite.

[PHILLIPS disappears into the hut. Spectators gasp in shock at
this affront. A moment later KALANIOPU emerges, followed
by PHILLIPS and the two boys.]

KALANIOPU:
Aloha!

COOK:
Greetings, Majesty.

[COOK takes him by the arm. More gasps.]

Random:
Kapu!

PHILLIPS:
Captain…

COOK:
We would like t' invite Your Majesty
Aboard the *Resolution* as our guest.
There are some matters that we must discuss.
I trust you won't refuse our hospitality.
You would oblige us greatly. Will you come?

KALANIOPU:
[Aside] I feel sinister currents in his voice,
Yet there's no reason they would wish me ill. –
I'll go.

COOK:
We have our boat to take you there.

[They march him towards their boat. A crowd of apprehensive
Hawaiians grows ever greater. It includes MANOA, the
KAHUNA, the King's wife KEAHE and others.]

Why knots this crowd?

Random:
They want to take our King!

KALANIOPU:
He does but want to speak to me.

[KALANIOPU's wife breaks out of the crowd.]

KEAHE:
Don't go
They mean you harm. They're holding Lani still.

KALANIOPU:
Kaimi's daughter?

190

KEAHE:
                          Yes. They want you next.

    COOK:
Your safety I myself will guaranty.

        KALANIOPU:
Why would he wish me wrong?

        KEAHE:
                              I beg you, stay.

    COOK:
What's happening? Is she his wife?

        KALANIOPU:
                              I'll go.

        KEAHE:
No, don't!

        COOK:
            Come on! Let's move!

        KEAHE:
                              They're taking him!
    COOK:
For Heaven's sake!

        PHILLIPS:
                    It looks like trouble, sir.

[Enter BEAUMONT. The crowd falls silent.]

        BEAUMONT:
You think I'm worth a king? A price too high.
You wanted only me. Let them go free.

COOK:
Lord Beaumont? I am Captain James Cook,
A British naval officer.

BEAUMONT:
                    Where is she, cur?

COOK:
Where's who?

BEAUMONT:
                    O, torture me no more!
I'll go in this. [Points at canoe] You bring her in your
                                        [launch,
And then we can exchange at th' halfway mark.

COOK:
I cannot fathom what you speak of, sir.
We came ashore to gain a boat's return.
A cutter has been stolen, t' our concern.
I want it back.

BEAUMONT:
                    And I, I want my daughter back.

COOK:
I haven't got her!

BEAUMONT:
                    Do not jest with this.
I want my daughter back!

COOK:
                    Your daughter?

BEAUMONT:
                                        Aye!

COOK:
And you believe I have her?

BEAUMONT:
'Course you do!
The message in the sand…

A Marine:
He has gone mad.

BEAUMONT:
Please, give her back to me, and then I'll go.

COOK:
I've never seen your daughter, nor have I
In all my life upon this beach set foot.

BEAUMONT:
What is your purpose hamming this pretence?

COOK:
Your anger's misdirected. I am not to blame.

BEAUMONT:
Manoa, let them not retreat!

PHILLIPS:
Captain, we must leave at once. 'Tis peril.

MANOA:
Where have you hidden her, you swines?

COOK:
Get back!

[MANOA moves towards him.]

MANOA:
We'll cut your stricken hearts right out!

193

COOK:

I'm warning you!

[MANOA advances a bit more. COOK fires his musket, but to his surprise the bullet ricochets off MANOA's war mat.[11] MANOA laughs.]

MANOA:
Behind your smoke and crackle, there is no fire.

PHILLIPS:
Let's go. 'Tis gunpowder by candlelight!

COOK:
[To the boat at sea] Bring in the launch!

BEAUMONT:

You came across the seas,
With sails that hellish breaths filled out,
To get some paltry stones and claim my greying head
In hollow victory, you steal my only child,
And now you come ashore to mock me thus.

[BEAUMONT takes a club from one of the warriors]

You've wronged me more than I deserve.
I damn you to th' bottom of the sea,
You greed-scaled gargoyle, Captain Cook! Take that!

[BEAUMONT hits COOK on the back of the head. He falls face down. The Marines pile into their boat as the Hawaiians rush at them. Confusion and uproar. Exeunt Marines. Enter LANI, wet, teary-eyed and out of breath: she has swum and ran from Javeed's ship.]

---

[11] Worn as armour in inter-tribal battles.

194

MANOA:
Lani!

BEAUMONT:
My child! You're safe! They let you free?

MANOA:
[Aside] How did she get here? And in such a state!
That villain must have wronged her after all.

BEAUMONT:
You weep and shiver. What's been done to you?
Did they... Not that! O crime unpardonable,
The tender garden ravaged by hell-fire.
The sun must blush at this too loathsome deed.

MANOA:
The fury of a thousand storms!

2nd WOMAN:
Shame, shame!

BEAUMONT:
At least we got the scoundrel. There he lies.

[BEAUMONT turns over COOK for her to see his face. She shakes her head and keeps on crying.]

What? Do you not recognise him? You must!
Look, look again. Was it not he? Who was it then?

MANOA:
[Aside] He will remember it was I who said
That she was taken by these other men.
Betrayal is a thinning rope of lies,
'Twill stretch and stretch, but lets you fall in th' end.

BEAUMONT:
It must have been some lesser tar upon that tub.

195

[He points towards the *Resolution*. LANI shakes her head and
indicates a distinctive feature of JAVEED.]

> Javeed! Has he not left? Of course! ' Twas he!
> A curse upon that monster spat from hell!

>   MANOA:
> [Aside] It was Javeed. Kaimi knows it too.
> O grief and woe won't ever leave my side!
> My throne is sinking into mud.
> The net has come unravelled. I must leave at once,
> Kaimi in his rage will have me killed.
> And Lani... ah, I fall before them both!
> Javeed. He was to meet me in the glade.
> I'll go there now.

[Exit MANOA]

>   BEAUMONT:
> [To NOHEA and other women]
> Take her hence and comfort her. Poor child!

[Exit LANI with NOHEA, the TWO OLD WOMEN and others]

> But whom has false suspicion rashly slain?
> Not guilty of the crimes I nailed on him.
[BEAUMONT examines COOK's body]
> He lives! Let him not die! He must be saved!

>   KAHUNA:
> [Aside] For then you will be saved yourself.

>   BEAUMONT:
> [To the KAHUNA] Go, summon up the life-sustaining
>   [force of plants,
> Your witching juices and concoctions. Go!

[Exit the KAHUNA]

196

He must be saved. Ah! Th' eyes regain their blue.
He lives. The startling way he has survived
Almost gives me faith in higher justice,
Yet that same justice aims its sword at me.
Did you come here for my arrest?

> COOK:

No, my voyage hither is exploration.

> BEAUMONT:

Then I have erred so many times on your account,
My tongue would dry before I told it all.
Accursed blood that ever boils too fast!
I've bid them do their best to guard your life,
But speak, for words are proof of life and sense
And I've not heard our language echo other tones
Than mine. For one, how do you know my name?

> COOK:

Your deeds have all been carved in legend now.
You are a story told in portside inns
And sailors' quarters, myth that colours out
The long, drab journey's flow. I know of you.

[Enter the KAHUNA with a small pot]

> KAHUNA:

This fluid will help.

> BEAUMONT:
> No, wait, wait. You drink first.

> KAHUNA:

Me?

> BEAUMONT:

Each new blow that I have taken has,

197

Like acid, marred away my faith in men.
I trust no one, not ev'n my shadow. Drink.
[The KAHUNA drinks. BEAUMONT nods and takes the pot.]
Leave us.

[Exeunt omnes, save BEAUMONT and COOK]

        It seems you are a Northerner.

    COOK:
I hail from Marton, in the Cleveland hills.

    BEAUMONT:
'Tis but ten miles from th' Beaumont country seat.

    COOK:
Indeed. I glimpsed your father there few times.

    BEAUMONT:
My father?

    COOK:
        Aye. I well remember him.

    BEAUMONT:
But tell me of yourself. For if you die,
I want to know who was the man I killed,
And if you live, no doubt 'twill make me glad
I did not halt so curious a life.

    COOK:
I'm fifty years old.

    BEAUMONT:
        How odd. Same age as I.

    COOK:
My father was a farmer, salt o' the earth,

198

But sea-salt was what my life came to spice.
I started out on ships that carry coal
From Whitby to the South, and then the Navy.
My first real voyage was t' America.
I sailed around Newfoundland, Nova Scotia
And at the age of forty I was picked
By the Royal Society to lead
An expedition to these Southern Seas
T' observe the passage of the Morning Star.
That rarest astronomical event
Occurs just once in every century
And we were privileged to see it pass.
We journeyed on to what the Dutch have called
The islands of New Zeeland, mapped and charted them,
Thence to New Holland's eastern coast
Which for a strange familiarity,
And th' homesickness that gnaws at all who sail
So arduously long, I named as New South Wales.
My second navigation was to find
Where th' fabled *Terra Australis* lies,
The Southern Land professed since ancient times
To be so great it poised the half we know.
I proved them wrong. There were no endless plains
Except those chained in timeless ice and frost.
Throughout these cautious glides across the map
We touched upon a panoply of isles.
There's not a thing that thrills my blood as much
As hearing shrill the shout of 'Land Ahoy!'
And seeing first those rocks where humans roost
Upon the scope of Nature's canvas blue.
And all those islands far apart
With all their landmarks, animals and plants,
With all their people, languages and rites,
So isolated that they seem immune to age…
They make it hard to disbelieve in God.
Creation is more endless variant
Than soaring fancy ever dares surmise.
Approaching some new place, from humble reefs

To many others long inhabited,
We can there never guess the landing scene:
We're creatures that defy their explanations,
Emerging from a place their thoughts don't roam.
Will we be seen as gods or dinner, or
Perchance more reasonably in between.
It often eases naming these new lands:
I gave the Friendly Islands that sweet name
To celebrate their nature on their map.
But I have also lost a launch of men
To th' heathen practice of devouring them.
My third of journeys was to find
Th' elusive North West Passage, but it proved
Another ancient wisdom loudly burst.
'Tis then I steered back here, for of these parts
What we know is but a drop in th' ocean.
We landed at another part of th' island,
A broken mast then forced us to return.
And that's my life, at least what fits my breath.
If one supposes this was for esteem,
They widely miss what spurred my wanderlust.
Those Dutchmen, Spaniards and Portuguese
Were men of most praiseworthy bravery
To ride beyond horizons into mystery,
Their maps as starkly white as were their sails,
But lacked of science in their travelling.
The shrunken brains of bygone centuries,
Had sought to put the unknown in a sack.
But Galileo, Magellan, Copernicus
Undid the sack to show what it concealed,
And force the world to stumble towards truth.
I studied navigation, shipbuilding,
Cartography, astronomy and algebra,
Discovery's a science as precise
As any one of these. I needed them
To fully master all the ocean's moods,
To guess its currents, rule its roaring storms.
I've sailed with botanists, astronomers

And draughtsmen, keen to learn from all of them.
The sun and moon like angels look on ships,
And those who fitly pray will guidance get.
But for that Mass, one needs mechanic priests.
I speak, of course, of our chronometers,
And lunar observations that keep time.
The choice of ship should neither be decried:
It might divide survival from demise.
[Points weakly towards the *Resolution* and *Discovery*]
Would you believe those two are common coaling
[ships?
Just like the ones I was apprenticed on.
They're slow as cattle; sturdy, low and wide,
There is no gale that can unseat their ride
Nor reef that can their belly scrape or harm.
I like to call them 'oxen of the sea.'
And when the ship is right, so too must be the food.
For th' hungry, knowledge is a bitter scrap.
How dearly paid those old adventurers!
They crawled into their ports of origin
As boats of ghosts, with half the crew long dead.
I vowed I'd never captain crafts like that,
To be a Charon of such ships of death,
And painted scurvy out with Nature's greens.
Success resides in preparation, not in skill or chance.
And I dare say, I've seen more of the world
Perhaps than any other living man.
Though fifty years may appear short,
It gives me comfort they were well employed.
I'm ready now t' explore the Seas Beyond...

BEAUMONT:
Strands of life so strangely spun together.
We were born almost side by side, and sailed
Between the same blue sea and same blue sky,
Yet never met until we're both so aged
And both undone by this selfsame intrigue.
We are each other's images, with me

201

The twisted image 'neath the rippling surface.
I could have been like you. I could have been...
These exiled years I only had one wish,
One blesséd thing that would have smoothed my brow:
The dove of peace in flight above these skies.
Of course, some wars could not averted be
I did my very best to make them soft.
It was some crude atonement that I sought,
Yes I, once coalman to the Underworld
Now blocked with force the chimney leading there.
Alas, a new Charybdis sucks me down:
My past. It clamours in my bursting skull,
It fills that private cell of no escape.
I was a great and able man,
Made blind and lame by guilt that swelled with age,
Like countless waves, so powerful and proud
Besieging the eternal shore
That only makes them drain to nothingness
As they retreat in meekening defeat,
A futile force now old and weak, with nought achieved.
I drowned into myself. I disappeared...
[COOK coughs and struggles to get up]

COOK:
I need some water.

BEAUMONT:
Water! Fetch some fast.

[Enter NOHEA with water. COOK drinks and coughs more.]

You must be moved from out this parching heat.
Go, call some men to take him to my hut.

[Exit NOHEA, enter Three Men]

Man:
We need another.

202

Man 2:
                    Where is Manoa?

        Man:
He's gone.

BEAUMONT:
Manoa gone? Where did he go?

        Man:
I do not know.

        BEAUMONT:
                    Did anyone see where?

        Man 3:
Towards the glade, I think.

        BEAUMONT:
                        'Twas he who said
That Lani had been taken to Cook's ship.
And now a most abrupt departure. Passing odd!
He knows a guilty share of this affair,
And must be found. [To Three Men] You, bear him
                        [where I dwell.
Treat him just like me, nay, even better.
I've almost read the book of life to th' end
But dread to see the final chapter's wend.

[Exeunt the Three Men carrying COOK, exit BEAUMONT in
another direction]

[Enter MANOA]

MANOA:
What have I done? What cross-eyed fool am I?
I've pandered her for whom I'd willing die,
I've made Kaimi wound, perhaps to death,
A man who's innocent. And all for what?
To speed the pace of what the gods ordained?
Unworthy vessel of my royal blood!
I've been a loathsome lackey to my greed.
Ambition's steps are always slippery,
Instead of one step up, I took two down.
I let the current lead to this cascade,
But came in a canoe steered by Javeed.
How could he...? She who's mute and cannot cry,
Whose nature's gentle as a little bird's,
Always thoughtful, loving of her father.
O, when I saw her face awash with tears,
My instinct whispered sordid truths at once.
I even sensed this end as I agreed.
And what of that man they say is Lono?
No doubt a man of greatness arching high
If he commands a fleet of ships so vast.
His blood bestains my hands as well.
Yet all this circles back to one: Javeed.
Javeed, the shadow that has choked us all.
He must be made to pay for murder, rape.
I'll kill him – in atonement and revenge,
For then I'll face a death of lesser shame
Yes, he's the one who most deserves the blame.
I hear him coming now.

[Enter JAVEED]

JAVEED:
Greetings, my boy.

204

Has all gone well?

MANOA:
                  Yes. All has gone.

JAVEED:
                                  Eh? Gone?
How's that?

MANOA:
Where are your guards?

JAVEED:
                        I left them by.
'Tis better they don't taste our words.
But tell me, in the Devil's name, what passed?

MANOA:
Beaumont stabbed the foreign chief.

JAVEED:
                              He can't have!
Did I misjudge him so? That cannot be!
He seemed so tamed, abhorring blood like poison.

MANOA:
And Lani has escaped captivity.
[JAVEED backs away]
Her muteness did accuse with eloquence.

JAVEED:
It wasn't me. I swear it wasn't me!

MANOA:
Then who?

JAVEED:
                  One of my seamen guarding her.

Licentious rogue. I had him flayed, of course.
I'll hand him over to you if you wish.

[Enter BEAUMONT]

BEAUMONT:
So! Vile and viler furtively entwined,
This coarse conspiracy confirmed at last!
If only I had guessed this plot before,
Before the Heavens bent above this isle.
Javeed, you loathsome, base-born basilisk!
Manoa, you I ask the word I dread, why?
You could have breathed the dream of common men:
The fairest wife, the post of chiefly might.
Your courage would have served you well in battles,
[why?

MANOA:
There are some deeds we do not choose, instead
We do not choose to check their fateful flow.
I find no reason now that stands debate,
But then, so many subtle hints and words
Connived to shape a most convincing whole.

JAVEED:
[Aside] This moment's fire purges each of us,
So let me spread it as it should be spread,
And exit in a puff! – I'm sure you feel
A granite weight to meet a traitor thus
And realise you've known him all along.

MANOA:
Quiet!

BEAUMONT:
What precisely was your part in 't?

MANOA:
He wanted you to think that Lono took your child.

206

JAVEED:
And he agreed! He let me have her!

MANOA:
Dog!
You promised me that she would not be harmed!

JAVEED:
He wanted riddance of your kind and you.

MANOA:
I didn't! Not of her!

JAVEED:
Of course you did!
It is so natural to hate you, Beaumont:
Your power, greed, manipulative ways.
Manoa hates you just as much as I.
That fullest hate is what united us,
The wish to tip your haughty edifice.
He spied on you to find your secrets out.
He stole the English boat to stir them up.
He went along with me most eagerly!

MANOA:
Enough, you bloody liar! You tricked me through!

JAVEED:
And you're a scurvied coward to deny your part!

[MANOA snatches JAVEED's knife and stabs him]

MANOA:
Die! Die, you worm!

BEAUMONT:
No! Stop!

JAVEED:

Too late. I'm done.

You've lost life's parry, for in death I better you.

[Dies]

BEAUMONT:

He's dead! And killed by you! Oh God!

MANOA:

It needed to be done, and you would not.

BEAUMONT:

First blood in Paradise. First blood in Paradise!
I'm doubly struck with murder and deceit,
Winded of my senses...

MANOA:

It needed to be done!

BEAUMONT:

My only noble wish desired but peace,
A futile sand-grain in a flood of blood.
The gentle dove with tar-dipped arrows downed.
O grief! The first blood shed in Paradise.
But there was nothing said of second blood...
The first blood spilt is death, but after that?
For Cook, though weakened is alive, but you,
You deserve the worst that weapons can inflict.
You have betrayed me, sold your people out,
You gave my daughter into torture's claws,
But it's yourself that you have wronged the most.

MANOA:

Kill me.

BEAUMONT:

Here's the steel of thirty pieces.

[Stabs him]

If only there had been someone to do
Alike with me when I was at your age,
It would have been a blest deliverance,
Mercy from a lifetime's troop of torment's shades.

[MANOA dies. Enter the KAHUNA and others]

KAHUNA:
The gods will be most pleased.

BEAUMONT:
Did you hear all?

KAHUNA:
[Nods] We bring you news of th' foreign chieftain's
[death.
'Twas you who first spilt blood in "Paradise."
He died soon after you left him.

BEAUMONT:
Before Javeed?
What rusting irony has spiked my fate!
I wished to warrant peace with threat of death,
But I was first to break the rule I wrought.
How fragile is this life! How quickly finished!
No second chance, nor court whereto appeal,
Our exit from this plane as wondrous as our start.
One can't accustom to the grinning sickle,
Life's seasons never seem indifferent.
Did Captain Cook breathe any final words?

KAHUNA:
He said, "Don't tell them this is how I died.
Let not a too dramatic death cast shade
On more noteworthy things that went before.
I don't desire my epitaph to read:
'The last great pirate's last great victim.'"

BEAUMONT:

Aye.

Our fates so eerily together chained:
Killing him I uttered mine own sentence.
It will be done just as he wanted it:
We'll tailor history to snugly fit.

[Exeunt omnes]

Act V

[Tech FX: The theatre's heating is turned progressively up during this act.]

[Music: Vivaldi's Violin Sonata Opus 2, Number 12, first movement.]

[The luakini heiau, sacrificial temple of the gods. Enter BEAUMONT, the KAHUNA, King KALANIOPU, LANI (restrained by the Two OLD WOMEN) and many others. A dais representing a sacrificial altar stands centre.]

BEAUMONT:
I will not rage at fate nor bargain seek.
I'm parched by drought of words, and all I feel
Is numbness blunt and strange, dolorous weight...
I've slain a man much greater than myself,
And with that widened still the breach 'tween us.
In him I also killed a part of me,
Destroyed a thing I've never found but always sought.
Though Fortune smiled with grace upon my birth,
I never smiled back, nor gave her thanks.
So many buds and shoots, now wilted all
By winds that howl from out th' abysmal gap
Between the possible and actual.
An oceanful of opportunities

210

Has trickled through my fingers into void.
Yet any drop of these I could have used as ink
And writ with it in steady hand my name
On history's grand page: one of the great.
What general I could have been! Or more,
The best explorer, Atlas of our times.
A modern Jason or Odysseus!
Instead, my name was written in the sand,
Thus the prophetic grains arranged themselves.
Damnation came for me before my death!
"A ship, when 't sails across the frothing waves
No trace behind it leaves. 'Twas same with me,
Who did, as soon as born, begin to end,
And left with no accomplishments to show,
But was consumed by his own wickedness."[12]
Now let this irksome circle be complete.
[Mounts the dais]

KALANIOPU:
You have my pardon. There's no call for this.

BEAUMONT:
You'll hew a brazen hypocrite of me?
If I accept what's coming, you must too.
My resolve is set as iron.
As for the gems that burnt and cut us all,
That fortune's place of sleep no one will learn.
Old Proteus shall lock it 'tween his teeth
And with its weight sink quicker to his crypt!
        "When one, it has but one.
        When two, each too has two
        But when there's three or more,
        Each still has three and never four."
To know, or least suspect, life's mystery
And know that one has missed the mark,
That is a keener ache and agony

---

[12] Wisdom of Solomon 5:10, 5:13 paraphrased

Than never having known where one has failed.
[To LANI] Forgive me, child. Forgive me everything.
[To the KAHUNA] Strike true. Miss not.
[The KAHUNA stabs him ceremonially]
                              I couldn't have wished for more,
And less would not have been enough.
[Dies. LANI breaks away and rushes to his body.]

KALANIOPU:
Come, child. It had to be. He wanted it.
Your father had a force of mana[13] in him.
When so much spirit's locked within one man,
It will with sureness come to burst its vessel.

[Enter CLERKE and Marines]

CLERKE:
[To KALANIOPU] Sir, as the Captain of th' *Discovery*,
It is my most desolate of duties
To have to ask you to release th' remains
O' my friend and mentor Captain James Cook,
Late prime of leaders and of navigators,
And best of sailors that I've ever known.

KALANIOPU:
That will be difficult, but I will try.
All nations share respect for the deceased.

CLERKE:
I see a certain justice has been served.
Who knows where he departed from the right?
Had he not fallen, then he might have sailed
Mayhap on greater waves than even Cook.
Fate's mockery for two such men of sea
To seal their destinies upon dry land!
Survived they reefs and storms, but not each other…

---

[13] The Polynesian concept of the human spirit.

Let us return t' our ships, and to a world
That's infinitely poorer for its loss.

[Exeunt omnes, save LANI]

LANI:
I cannot speak, but I'm not mute in thought,
Though now I'd silence that as well, for then
I would not have to taste the palping pain
Of both a father and a lover lost.
I'd add myself atop this corpses' heap,
But those who live must shoulder life for others dead.

A man who on the highest mountain trod
Can still be discontent to not reach God.
To aim for greatness is the noblest human end:
To vanquish time, by matching it in stride,
Defeat the hydra-heads of multiplying years,
Be immortal, extraordinary!
But if the only greatness one can reach
Is one that suckles guilt when it's reviewed?
Man's the halfway mark 'tween God and Devil.
At least that's how, as babes, our journey starts.
Which way the yard-arm swings is up to us.
But every age will map to its own scale
The distance and direction to these two:
The ancient virtue rusts to modern vice,
And shines again when comes its season back.
No, one can never know how they'll be judged,
Their greatness may be damned by times to come.
The drive to rise is tempered by uncertainty.
And so, we're ground between a bland obscurity
Or risking all for grand ideals' sake.
There's one thought I wish I could have told them:
Perhaps 'tis less a torment to believe
The greatest thing that one can do… is live.

[Curtain]

213

Finis

LaVergne, TN USA
25 July 2010
190787LV00002B/1/P

9 780646 527215